W.i.t.c.h.

Will   Irma   Taranee   Cornelia   Hay Lin

A Different Path

Adapted by ELIZABETH LENHARD

HarperCollins *Children's Books*

This book was first published in the USA in 2004 by Volo/Hyperion Books for Children
First published in Great Britain in 2005 by HarperCollins *Children's Books*, a division of
HarperCollins Publishers Ltd.

© 2006 Disney Enterprises, Inc.

ISBN 13 978-0-00-720948-4
ISBN 0-00-720948-7

1 3 5 7 9 10 8 6 4

The HarperCollins website is:
www.harpercollinschildrensbooks.co.uk

Visit www.clubwitch.co.uk

Printed and bound in Italy

ONE

Taranee followed Will, Irma, and Hay Lin out of Cornelia's apartment building. She was glad the doorman was waiting in the sleek lobby to usher the girls through the glass door. She was so shaken she doubted she could have gotten a grip on the door's shiny chrome handle.

She couldn't believe that Cornelia had turned on her friends – after all they'd been through together!

Irma, of course, was less troubled than Taranee. She brushed her fingers through her brown hair and gazed casually into the sunny Heatherfield sky.

"Well, we gave that talk with Cornelia our best shot," Irma said to her girlfriends breezily. "Didn't go so hot, did it?"

Will stalked up to Irma, her face red with anger.

"It would've gone better if you hadn't said those things to her," Will scolded. "What were you thinking?"

Irma stared at Will with wide, shocked, blue eyes.

"Now *you're* yelling at me, too?" she said in disbelief.

"Of course, I am," Will replied. "You were too hard on Cornelia. She's completely depressed, and we should be trying to help her."

Irma's face grew serious. "*You* should be helping her, because I've had it with this whole story!" she sniffed.

Taranee gasped, covering her mouth with her hand. She watched Irma stomp down the pavement.

First Cornelia bails on us, she thought in alarm. And now Irma!

Hay Lin clearly wasn't happy about the new turn of events, either.

"Irma, wait!" she yelled to Irma's back.

Irma continued to storm away. Hay Lin began to trot after her, glancing back at Will and Taranee as she went.

"I'll try to calm her down," she said with a shrug. "Talk to you later."

"Good luck," Will muttered.

Taranee waved good-bye to Hay Lin. If anybody could talk Irma out of her funk, Taranee thought with a sigh, it's Hay Lin. Not only is she the most free-spirited girl in our group, she's also Irma's best friend. She always laughs at Irma's jokes, no matter how goofy they are. And Irma always has a nice word to say about Hay Lin's latest art project or fashion design. They understand each other completely.

Sort of like me and *my* best friend, Taranee thought, looking up to glance at Will. We understood each other from the first moment we met. Probably because we were both nervous new kids at the Sheffield Institute.

After school that first day, Will and Taranee had biked home together, and they had totally bonded.

And then, that night at the Halloween dance, Taranee remembered with a grin, they had hung out with Irma, Cornelia, and Hay Lin. That was when their group had really taken shape.

It was also, Taranee recalled with a shiver, when all their troubles had begun.

An image of Elyon – who had once been the girls' classmate and Cornelia's best friend – flashed through Taranee's mind. She could see Elyon's pale blue eyes and long braids of the exact same pale-gold colour as straw.

Halloween, Taranee recalled, was Elyon's last night in Heatherfield. That was the night she had gone to Metamoor.

Metamoor was the world lurking just beyond ours, Taranee thought. Only none of us knew it existed, because it was hidden behind the Veil.

We eventually learned that the Veil was a cosmic barrier – invisible and undetectable – placed between the earth and Metamoor by a powerful being known as the Oracle of Candracar. He was wise and all-knowing, and he exuded peace.

The Oracle also knew that Metamoor was going to be a major trouble spot in the universe.

It hadn't always been that way. Once, Metamoor had been a happy place. Green-skinned, talking lizards, cobalt-blue giants, bulky beings with red eyes and dreadlocks had lived in stone turrets and thatched-roof cottages in a city called Meridian. They had lived under the benevolent reigns of a long line of queens; only women had been allowed to rule the land of Metamoor, and they always had – until an evil presence had tried to thwart that tradition.

That evil presence was a young man – a prince, actually. He was the only son of Meridian's king and queen and the older brother of Meridian's princess, a girl who was destined one day to rise to power and assume the title of Light of Meridian.

The prince's name was Phobos. And his younger sister?

Her name was Elyon.

Elyon, who'd grown up in Heatherfield as an ordinary girl, was actually the princess of Metamoor – the Light of Meridian. And the whole time she lived in Heatherfield, Elyon had had no idea that she possessed this secret identity and destiny.

She'd been a baby when her parents died. Soon after that tragedy, Prince Phobos had hatched a horrible plan to steal Elyon's magical powers, and with them, her young life.

He would have succeeded if three individuals hadn't stepped in. Elyon's nanny and two army commanders had taken the infant queen and brought her to the earth. Once there, the Metamoorians had transformed their scaly bodies into human ones. The commanders had posed as Elyon's parents, calling themselves Thomas and Eleanor Brown, and Elyon's nanny had become a Sheffield Institute math teacher named Mrs. Rudolph.

Together, the trio of protectors had raised Elyon to be a normal girl from Heatherfield.

Meanwhile, the Oracle had created the Veil, to keep Phobos from finding Elyon and to keep the peace. Elyon had grown up ignorant of her true identity, while Phobos had grown more and more bitter.

He had ruled over Metamoor with cruelty and terror and drained that world of its magical energy. Under the prince's rule, Metamoor had become a cold, unforgiving place.

Everybody in Meridian had lived without hope – until the millennium struck.

And *then*, Taranee thought as she leaned against a lamppost on the pavement, things began to get really interesting.

The Veil began to tear, creating twelve holes. Those holes became portals – tunnels that connected Meridian to Heatherfield – allowing Cedric, Phobos's servant, to slither through and lure Elyon to Meridian.

But Elyon wasn't Phobos's only prey. The open passageways left countless other Heatherfielders in danger.

So the Oracle appointed five young girls to protect the portals – to become Guardians of the Veil.

Will, Irma, Cornelia, Hay Lin, and I are those Guardians, Taranee thought proudly. Our names even form an acronym – W.I.T.C.H.!

The girls had more than just a catchy group title, though. The Oracle had given them powers with which both to fend off Metamoorian bad guys and close the portals.

Each girl's power controlled a different element. Hay Lin, a free spirit, had power over the air. Grounded Cornelia was the group's earth girl, conjuring up images in tree leaves, blasting holes in brick walls, or inventing quick-growing vines with a twitch of her magic fingers.

Irma, who could have spent every night of the week soaking in long, hot baths, wielded her magic over water.

And me, Taranee thought with a twinkle in

her eye and a burst of pride. I play with fire.

That left Will. Taranee looked over at her friend sitting in the grass. Will was the Keeper of the Heart of Candracar, a shimmery, crystal orb. Whenever the Guardians were in a pinch, Will called upon the orb and then released the pink amulet from the palm of her hand. It blasted all five girls with extra magical oomph, helping them turn into the most powerful beings possible.

It also transformed their appearances in a major way! In their Guardian guises, the girls looked older. Their bodies went from flat to curvy in one instant. Their usual jeans, fleeces, and sneakers were replaced by midriff-baring halter tops, purple-and-turquoise-striped leggings, and colourful boots. They even sprouted wings.

We are a pretty *amazing* team! Taranee thought. Not only did we close most of the portals in the Veil, we also helped Elyon defeat Prince Phobos! The moment Elyon took her rightful place on Meridian's throne, things began looking up for the city. The sun broke through the clouds, the grass grew greener.

Elyon and her adoptive parents, Taranee remembered happily, were able to start settling into the royal palace and were setting out to establish a new, happier era in Meridian. And to make sure things *stayed* happy, the Oracle banished Phobos and Cedric to the faraway Tower of Mists, and dissolved the Veil.

Which means we are free of our Guardian duties! Taranee thought exultantly. At least, for now. The Oracle warned us that he might need us again.

Maybe *free* isn't exactly the right word, Taranee corrected herself silently, reflecting upon Cornelia. Cornelia probably feels anything but free. She's lost her best friend. I mean, Elyon might be safe, but she's also so far away. She belongs in Metamoor now, which means her friendship with Cornelia can never be the same again.

And her true love, Caleb? Well, he'll never be the same again, either.

Caleb had been a Murmurer once. Most Murmurers lived to serve Phobos. They were sleepless, emotionless, thoughtless creatures.

Caleb, though, had been different.

With his comrades, Caleb had fought to restore Elyon to the throne and peace to Meridian. Along the way, he'd met Cornelia.

The rebel and the Guardian had fallen in love at first sight. It didn't matter that they had only seen each other in person a handful of times. They had seen one another plenty of times before, in their dreams. They were destined to be together.

Which made Phobos's actions all the more tragic, Taranee thought. The prince used his dark magic to turn Caleb back into his original form – a beautiful white flower.

If something like that ever happened to Nigel, Taranee went on thinking, I don't know what I would do!

Taranee felt herself blush at the thought of her own crush – brown-eyed, sweet Nigel. Meeting Nigel, and realizing he liked her as much as she liked him, had made Heatherfield more exciting to Taranee. The only thing more important to her was her bond with her four girlfriends.

A bond Taranee had thought of as unbreakable – until today.

Taranee's gaze turned to Will. Her knees were bunched up beneath her chin, and the corners of her mouth sagged in a frown.

"Now," Taranee said, trying to break into

Will's sulk. "What should we do to make this crummy afternoon better?"

"I don't know what we should do, Taranee," Will grumbled in reply. "I really don't know."

Without another word, Will pulled herself to her feet. Shoving her hands deep into her jeans pockets, she began to walk away.

Taranee stared after her.

Maybe, she thought with a shiver, Will is just tired of this whole Guardian gig. Maybe she wants to wash her hands of it – and us – completely!

Feeling her heart sink, Taranee began to walk toward the bus stop on the corner. She barely noticed the crowd of Heatherfielders dodging around her on the busy pavement as she slumped along.

What's happening to us anyway? she thought.

Taranee slouched against the bus-stop sign and looked down at the pavement until the bus came. She climbed into the bus slowly. The moment she pulled her fare card out of the fare box, the bus lurched away from the curb. Taranee stumbled, then grabbed for a pole in the aisle. She clung to it, struggling for balance.

Real friends should be able to solve their problems, she thought with a frown. So what are we doing? Maybe we were just kidding ourselves. Maybe we're just five strangers who stuck together out of fear. Now that the battle for Meridian is finally over, what's going to happen to us?

Will our friendship end as well?

TWO

After leaving Taranee in front of Cornelia's building, Will walked slowly home.

She wished that Taranee, Irma, Cornelia, or Hay Lin had been willing to lend a sympathetic ear, or even a comforting shoulder, as she bemoaned her bad day.

But they didn't, Will thought with a sigh. That figures, with a day like today.

Let's see, she thought. This morning, my pet dormouse chewed a hole in my favorite T-shirt, the bright yellow one with the frogs hopping up the sleeves.

Then, in history class, Mr. Collins sprang *another* pop quiz on us. And who was the first student he called on to answer some totally obscure question about the

Peloponnesian War? Me, of course! I'm sure it had absolutely *nothing* to do with the fact that Mr. Collins is dating my mother and doesn't want to favor me in class.

Will cringed, picturing her mum holding hands with Mr. Collins over a candlelit table with cheesy music in the background.

Let's go ahead and add *that* to my bummer list: my mother is dating my history teacher! Ewww!

It wasn't as though Will didn't want her mum to date *at all*. Eventually, she knew that was going to happen. Will felt pretty much fine about the idea of her Mum dating. But did it *have* to be with a teacher? A teacher Will saw every day at *her* school, where there were other kids who might find out? It was too embarrassing. Too gross!

So, let's move on, Will thought, to the biggest bummer: the big fight with my best friends! Talk about an awful way to end the day.

By the time Will finally reached the door of her apartment building, she was wearing a stressed-out scowl.

Home, she thought irritably. Considering

the way my mum and I have been getting along lately – or *not* getting along, to be more accurate – being home might just be another bummer to add to the list.

Will took the elevator up to her floor and unlocked the front door. She headed straight for the kitchen.

I think a day like this calls for some major amounts of chocolate, she thought.

Before Will made it into the kitchen, though, she let out a squeak of surprise.

"Mum!" she said. "You're home early."

"Hi, Will!" her mum chirped. "I'm glad you're here. I wanted to talk to you about something."

Uh-oh, Will thought, noticing that her mother's face was paler than usual. When she started out like that, it always meant bad news. Will took a deep breath and, flopping into the big, soft couch in the living room, announced, "I'm all ears."

Her mum crossed her arms and began to pace back and forth in front of Will. It looked as though she were having trouble finding the right words. "I don't know how to tell you this," she said, with a wobble in her voice, "so I'll just say it. I gave my boss a request for a transfer."

Will's tongue suddenly felt like a block of wood, which explained why she couldn't scream, *What are you talking about? We can't move! It's a matter of life or death!*

The only thing Will *could* do was struggle for breath and cling to the couch cushions as her mother pressed nervously on.

"In June," she explained, "as soon as you've finished school, we're moving."

Will couldn't form any words with her mouth. She was scared she might burst into flames right then and there, setting the couch's cherry-red slipcover on fire, too.

That was when Will's calmer, cooler, Guardian self kicked in.

Did I just sit there like a lump, she asked herself, when Taranee was trapped in Phobos's palace, thinking her friends had forgotten her? No way! I led the rest of the Guardians to her rescue. We reunited and battled with our full power.

Did I just stand by when Cedric turned into a monster and tried to steal Elyon's Crown of Light? Will thought. Not even! Instead, I planted the cursed crown on the big bully's own head. It absorbed Cedric's powers and put an end to his evil plans to take over the throne. Which means I'm strong enough to stand up to my own mother, right? But I can't do that unless I get this mouth of mine to work already! I need to speak!

"B – but – but – but, WHY?" Will finally managed to yell.

"Because it'll be better for everyone," Mum said, pointing a stern finger at her daughter. "Especially for you! I'll be working at a different branch of Simultech, and you'll – "

She couldn't believe what her mother had just said. What was happening? There was no way she could leave Heatherfield.

Not to mention, her friends, or her destiny as a Guardian! No! Not only had all of those things finally made Will feel as though Heatherfield were home, they were keeping the world in one piece! The Oracle had ordered the Guardians to stay together, to stay ready.

"But I don't want to leave Heatherfield!" Will interrupted, crossing her arms stubbornly over her chest. "We just got here! And I can't leave!"

How would she be able to do that from hundreds of miles away?

If only Mum could understand, Will thought.

Tears sprang to her eyes.

Turning to look out the window, Will listened numbly as her mother chattered.

"I've tried to talk to you about it lots of times," her mum said with a quiver in her voice. "But over the last few months, you've been more and more distant. Maybe you haven't really settled in here – "

"And you think moving again would solve everything?" Will demanded, whirling away from the window to face her mother. "Why didn't we decide on this together? This is my life, too, you know." As she stopped talking, she felt a sob well up in her chest. But there was no way she could tell her mum the real reason. She couldn't say, "I am a Guardian of the Veil and I need to be near my Guardian friends!" Will swallowed her sob and steeled herself for her mother's response.

Reaching toward Will, her mum softened her voice. "We'll start over again somewhere else, honey. Maybe Heatherfield was just a bad choice."

"And what about Mr. Collins?" Will burst out. "Did you even think of him?" Ugh, Will thought. You *know* the situation is desperate when I'm taking sides with Mr. Collins! But, from the expression on Mum's face, it looks as if I've hit a nerve. Maybe that was a good move!

Will's mum slowly rested her head in her hands. For a minute, Will wondered if she were crying. She took a couple of deep breaths before she answered in a strained whisper.

"I haven't talked to Dean about this yet," she murmured sadly. She paused for a minute before continuing, as if the strain of the conversation were too much. "But he'll have to understand. I want you to be happy. I've made some mistakes over the last few months, and – "

"And you're about to make another one!" Will shouted as she turned her back on her mother and sprinted toward her room at the back of the apartment. She heard her mother running after her, so she quickened her pace and moved even faster. "I don't want to move away!" she yelled over her shoulder.

"Wait!" her mum cried. "Can't we talk this over calmly? Since we moved to Heatherfield, you've – you've changed. If it isn't because we moved here, then what is it? Please, help me understand, Will!"

Will shook her head so hard that her red hair slapped her cheeks and stung her eyes. There was nothing she could say that would make her mother understand. Anger gave way to sadness, and she couldn't stop the tears from coming. Wiping her eyes, she plunged into her bedroom and slammed the door in her mother's face.

"I can't stand talking to closed doors anymore!" her mum yelled.

Will flopped backward against the door with a thud, then slid to the floor. Hunching her knees up below her chin, she buried her face in her arms and sobbed.

Finally, she heard her mother's footsteps moving down the hall to her own bedroom.

This was what Will wanted – to be left alone. Wasn't it?

How can I tell you, Mum? she thought, tears streaming down her face. I can't tell you my secret. I can't tell you about the Heart of Candracar, or the Oracle. I can't tell you any of it! But if I don't do something, in a few months, the Guardians of the Veil won't exist any longer. And I have to tell *someone* that. But who? I really need a friend right now!

Her eyes still blurry with tears, Will groped in her sweatshirt pocket for her cell phone. She was still crying as she hit the first button on the speed-dial pad. She was calling someone who would understand what she was feeling. Someone who might know what to do. At least, Will hoped so.

THREE

Beeep! Beeep! Beeep!

Taranee glanced into her living room, where the phone was ringing insistently.

Weird, she thought with a frown. I never noticed how *incredibly* annoying our phone sounds. Then again, everything sounds pretty annoying at the moment. Especially . . .

"No, Taranee! I don't want to discuss this again!"

. . . My mother, Taranee thought with a groan.

Taranee's arms were crossed sullenly over her chest as her mother stated her case. Normally, Taranee had to admit, her mum's arguments were pretty solid. But today, the woman was being completely unreasonable!

"I'm telling you for the last time," her mum announced sternly, "I don't like your seeing that boy, Nigel!"

With her blunt-cut, blue-black hair and angry, dark eyes, her mother couldn't have looked more severe. Even so, Taranee managed to issue a retort. "Nigel's just a friend, Mum! *And* he's a nice guy!"

Her mum's face softened a bit. Taranee braced herself. An outsider might have thought the change in her mother's expression was a good sign, but Taranee knew better. At that very moment, Judge Cook was deep in thought, formulating the perfect response to Taranee's protest.

As Taranee waited for her mother's verdict, she glimpsed her brother, Peter, loping over to the living-room phone, which was still ringing. He picked it up.

"Hello? Oh, hi, Will. I'm just fine, and you?" he said.

After a pause, Peter peered through the big, square doorway between the sun-filled living room and the kitchen.

"Well," he said, "I guess you could say that Taranee's home, but right now, she's busy talking with our mum. And I get the impression they won't be done for quite a while."

Whatever gave you *that* impression, Peter? Taranee thought sarcastically.

Taranee sighed as Peter hung up the phone and moved into the kitchen doorway. Slouching against the doorjamb, he gazed at his feuding mother and sister with a bemused grin.

Great, Taranee thought. Now we have an audience. This is going from bad to worse. I can't talk to my best friend on the phone, Peter's laughing at me, and my mum is being *totally* unfair.

The most frustrating part was that Taranee knew exactly why her mother was being so stubborn.

Judge Cook still hadn't forgiven Nigel for his mistake.

Taranee shook her head slightly. The Nigel she knew now was sweet and kind. It was hard to connect him with the boy he used to be or the boy her mum thought he still was.

She still thinks of him as a member of Uriah's gang.

As Nigel had explained to Taranee, he had

become a regular, if reluctant, accomplice to Uriah's mischief and troublemaking.

Until the day they'd gotten caught.

Taranee recalled with a pang of guilt what had happened that day. After hearing rumors of a monster lurking in the Heatherfield Museum, Uriah, Nigel, and Uriah's two lugs, Kurt and Laurent, had broken into the big building. Uriah had probably thought of the mission as a simple dare. After all, Uriah probably didn't believe in monsters.

Only Taranee and the other Guardians knew that the rumors were true! There actually had been a monster in the museum. It was Cedric, and he had once again come to Heatherfield to seek out – and destroy – the Guardians.

As it turned out, neither Cedric nor Uriah succeeded in their schemes that evening. When Kurt tripped off an alarm, Cedric dived back through his portal to Metamoor, and Uriah and company ended up being arrested by the police for breaking and entering.

They were sentenced by, of all people, Judge Cook. She ordered all four boys to do community service. And that was taking it easy on them. Taranee was pretty sure that if her mother had wanted, she could have given the boys a much harsher sentence.

Since then, Nigel no longer hung around with Uriah, and he and Taranee had started becoming closer with every passing day.

And now my mother wants to ruin all of that, Taranee thought indignantly.

"Since what happened at the museum, he's changed," Taranee said forcefully, "but you don't care! You've already made up your mind about him!"

"And what if I have?" her mum replied. "Outside of this house, I'm a judge and I'm impartial, but here, in my home, I have the right to my own opinion. And my opinion is *especially* important when it comes to my daughter's future and whom she chooses to hang out with. Nigel may be innocent, friendly, and cute, but I still don't like him!"

Taranee whirled around so fast, the long, beaded braid that dangled behind her left ear hit her glasses with a *thwack*. As she stomped back to her bedroom, she heard Peter's laid-back surfer's voice.

"So, Mum," he said. "You handed down

a sentence without a fair trial, eh?"

"Peter," her mother snapped back irritably, "what your sister needs isn't a defense attorney. She needs a bit of common sense!"

Taranee lowered her head. She wanted to blot out her mother's angry voice – and their entire conversation! She shot into her room and slammed the door.

If Mum thinks I'm going to stop hanging out with Nigel, she thought as she stomped toward the window, she'd better think again. How can she ask me to do something like that?

Taranee flopped into her favorite spot in the room – her window seat. With the green curtains thrown open, the bench was warm and inviting. Taranee settled into the cushion and slumped against the window frame with a snort of disgust.

"She doesn't know Nigel like I do," she grumbled. "If she did, she wouldn't even – huh?"

Out of the corner of her eye, Taranee had spotted movement in the yard just outside her window. It had looked too big to be a squirrel or raccoon.

Taranee twisted around in her seat and

peered out the window, her heart thumping.

There! She was right! She'd spotted a man. A very tall and broad-shouldered man, ducking into some bushes outside the low, brick fence that enclosed the Cooks' backyard.

"Who's out there?" Taranee whispered to herself. "I definitely saw somebody in the trees."

At that point, the old Taranee would have started trembling and run down the hallway to leap into her mother's arms.

But Nigel wasn't the only one who'd changed recently. The fire that had begun to burn in Taranee's fingers also burned in her belly, making her strong and fearless.

Taranee swung her windows open and vaulted lightly out on to the grass. She crept toward the wall and stared intently into the trees and bushes beyond her family's property line.

There was no one there.

But I'm sure, Taranee thought hesitantly. She shielded her eyes from the sun and looked harder. But when she still saw nothing, she shrugged.

No one, she thought, turning to walk back

toward her bedroom window. I must have imag
– Oh!

Taranee felt all the blood drain from her face – maybe even the entire upper half of her body! Luckily, her legs were still working, so she was able to run over to her window, where she fell to her knees.

On the red brick wall beneath Taranee's open window were some words scrawled in sticky, black paint.

Even more repugnant than the paint's tar-like stench were the words it spelled: *I KNOW WHO YOU ARE, TARANEE.*

Taranee gasped, then looked over her shoulder again. This time, she *did* tremble. Again, she scanned the backyard.

And again, she saw nothing.

Who would write this? Taranee wondered, turning back to look at the ugly scrawl. And what do they know about me?

I better get rid of this writing before someone else sees it, she thought breathlessly. Then I have to tell the others about it. Someone might have discovered our secret!

Holding her palm out toward the wall, Taranee closed her eyes and summoned her magic. She felt intense warmth well up in her body. It bubbled pleasantly into her chest, then sizzled down her arms to end up in the flat of her hand.

Ksssssssssss.

Taranee opened her eyes in time to see a cloud of orange-tinged smoke pour from her hand. It sizzled as fire hit the brick wall.

In mere seconds, the graffiti was gone, burned away by Taranee's strong magic.

With that done, Taranee jumped to her feet. She took one last apprehensive look at the woods before climbing back through the window into her bedroom.

First I'll call Will, she thought as she landed on the floor. And then Hay Lin. Oh, wait a minute.

Taranee sat down heavily on the window seat. She'd just realised something. Just then, out in the open air, she'd used her magic! Sure, she hadn't seen anybody around, but who knew? Maybe somebody had been there, hidden away, watching her every move!

What if this was all my fault? she wondered. The other Guardians would be so mad! Maybe I'd better just keep quiet and wait to see what happens next.

Filled with anxiety, Taranee made her way through a tense family dinner. Her mum was still irritated with her and didn't say much.

Then she sighed over her homework and went to bed early.

Tomorrow, Taranee thought as her weary head hit the pillow, tomorrow I can hopefully forget about all of this.

Lazily, Taranee opened one brown eye and glanced at her ticking bedside clock to see how much time she had left to sleep.

The minute hand was on the twelve, and the hour hand was on the – eleven?

Taranee's eye grew wide with shock.

"Oh, no!" she shrieked. "It's eleven o'clock! I'm superlate! My alarm didn't go off!"

Taranee leaped out of bed, sending her pink flannel sheets and her pretty, patchwork quilt flying. As she sprinted for the bedroom door, she yelled out, "Why didn't anyone wake me up?"

She stumbled down the hall, rubbing her eyes in bewilderment. She listened for an apologetic shout from her father in his basement office. Or her mother or brother.

"Mum!" she called out. "Dad? Peter?"

Taranee reached the kitchen door and peered inside. Instead of seeing her family, all she saw was the kitchen table, sparkling – and bare. The counters were wiped clean, the lights were off, and the coffeepot was empty.

"No one!" Taranee grumbled. "They've all left already. *And* they forgot about me. That's just great!"

Taranee glanced at the kitchen clock. It was two minutes past eleven.

Since I'm late already, she thought, I might as well take an extra fifteen minutes and have some breakfast. I'm starving!

Walking over to the refrigerator, Taranee rubbed her eyes once more. They felt swollen. She was exhausted.

Of course I am, she complained to herself. That message on the wall out there made it impossible for me to sleep. All I could do all night was think about who might have written that horrible message.

Taranee grabbed a jar of cherry jam and two slices of soft, white bread. She popped the bread into the toaster. As she waited, she stuck a knife into the jam jar and stirred the contents idly.

Maybe the graffiti is one of Irma's little pranks, she thought.

At the idea of Irma's sneaking into her backyard, one hand clutching a spray-paint can and the other clamped over her mouth to suppress her giggles, Taranee felt her spirits lift.

Of course! she told herself. This is just the kind of stunt Irma would pull on one of her friends.

The toast popped out, and Taranee began spreading the warm slices with jam.

I'd better ask Irma about this right away, she thought.

Happy with her plan, Taranee sat down at the kitchen table and took a big bite of her toast.

And that was when she heard the noise.

Klump!

Pausing in mid-bite, Taranee looked slowly and fearfully over her shoulder.

The heavy and ominous thump had come from Taranee's bedroom!

Taranee jumped out of her chair and darted to the kitchen doorway, peeking through it timidly. She saw nothing but the long, empty hallway and the closed door of her own room.

Rubbing her hands together nervously, Taranee began to tiptoe down the hall.

Maybe something just fell, she told herself as she crept along. Maybe the wind made that noise.

When Taranee reached the end of the hall, every muscle in her body seemed to want her to spin around and run in the opposite direction. But she grabbed the knob and pushed the door open. Holding her breath, she peeked into her room.

Phew! Taranee thought with a sheepish smile. I'm just being a chicken! No one's in here.

Taranee took a cautious step into her room. As her hand left the knob, the door swung slowly on its hinges, making a *creeeaaak* sound.

The hairs on the back of Taranee's neck stood up, and she felt herself go on the alert. She scanned her room suspiciously, not sure exactly what she was looking for. A strange shape beneath her sheets? An ominous shadow in the corner? Or –

"Aaaaaghhh!" Taranee shrieked.

Make that, some red paint scrawled on the inside of the open door of her armoire!

Gasping, Taranee ran toward the graffiti. Without her glasses on, she had to get frighteningly close to the writing before she could make out its message:

I KNOW WHO YOU ARE!

"No!" Taranee cried, covering her mouth with shaking hands.

Then she spotted something else.

Taped to the white surface of her armoire, just beneath the ugly graffiti, was a photo.

Taranee quickly grabbed the snapshot off the door. As she stared at the image, tears began to run down her cheeks.

"That's me in this photo!" she cried in horror.

In the photo, her face was half buried in her pillow. Her only visible eye was squeezed shut. And . . . she was wearing the very same pink tank top she had on now.

Somebody was in my room last night, Taranee thought, sinking to the edge of her mattress. And they took my picture while I was sleeping!

Through a haze, she looked at the shelf that

normally housed her camera collection.

Her camera was on the left side of the top shelf, not the left side of the *middle* shelf, the spot where Taranee normally always put it.

It's not in its usual place, she told herself. This can't be happening!

Still struggling from the shock of what she'd seen, she scooped her jeans up from the floor and blindly grabbed a green sweater out of her closet. She quickly dressed and sprinted out of the house.

I have to warn the others right away, she told herself as she quickly slammed the front door shut and ran toward her bike.

I should have told my friends about this graffiti last night, she thought, giving her pedals a mighty, leg-punishing push. I should have woken up earlier!

She continued to berate herself: I should have done something before it came to this. Any way you look at this situation, I didn't do enough.

As Taranee skidded around a corner, she caught sight of the Sheffield Institute. She didn't bother to lock up her bike when she arrived at the school. She simply sprinted toward the large wooden auditorium doors.

I just hope, she thought, that I'm not too late to help my friends!

FOUR

Hay Lin yawned and stretched as she walked into the Sheffield auditorium.

I couldn't sleep at all last night, because I was so bummed about that ugly scene at Cornelia's yesterday, Hay Lin thought as she was hit by another yawn. Then Will and Irma got into a fight on top of that! Not very Guardian-like, if you ask me! Even my parents could tell I was in a funk last night. And that is never a good sign.

She sighed. All those depressing thoughts were weighing her down. She knew she had to shake the gloominess from her head.

I can't let myself get any bluer about this, she thought scolding herself. Today will be better.

She walked into the school and faced the crowded Sheffield hallways with a smile. At least today was an assembly day and there would be no regular classes.

"Come on, kids! Keep moving!" Mrs. Knickerbocker bellowed.

The braying voice of Sheffield's principal startled Hay Lin. She turned around to see Mrs. Knickerbocker standing amidst a swarm of students. Thanks to her tall, beehive hairdo, she towered high above them.

"Come on!" she urged the droopy Sheffielders. "There are still some great seats in the front row. Don't all cower in the back!"

One thing you can say about Mrs. Knickerbocker, Hay Lin thought with a grimace. She's anything but subtle!

Suddenly, Hay Lin noticed Will emerge from the crowd looking overwhelmed. She scanned the room anxiously, as if searching for something. Relief crossed Will's face as she spotted Hay Lin. Will began to make her way toward her friend.

Who can blame her for being weirded out? Hay Lin thought. This is the most bizarre day of the year for Sheffielders. And it's also the only thing that could possibly make us regret our one chance to miss eight hours of classes!

Will arrived at Hay Lin's side and gave her a weak wave. Together, the girls moved into the auditorium, selected a row, and found a couple of seats behind Martin Tubbs.

Hay Lin had to smile when she saw Martin, with his big, round glasses falling off his nose. For years, it had seemed that wherever Irma went, Martin had appeared, popping out of the woodwork, calling Irma his little sweet potato and asking her on dates. His crush on Irma was nothing if not obvious.

Needless to say, Irma had always replied to Martin's declarations of love with scathing comebacks.

Hay Lin smirked. Clearly, Irma would have a good quip. She was the funniest girl Hay Lin knew. Well, usually. This morning, she was about as interesting as oatmeal.

Hay Lin peered across the auditorium. Irma was sitting in the middle of a row packed with students she barely knew. Even though they were practically strangers, she was laughing and talking to them as though they were her good friends. She'd already been in that seat when Hay Lin had arrived at the auditorium a few minutes earlier.

It's so weird, Hay Lin thought grumpily. Irma wasn't late to school today, or even on time. She was *early*, which *never* happens. Then she went and found a seat without me, and didn't even bother to save me a spot. And on *this* day, of all days!

Hay Lin slumped deeper into her own seat.

Last year, she thought, Irma made it her personal mission to crack me up throughout the long, dreary assembly. She kept up a running commentary on other kids' fashion faux pas and cracked jokes about the speeches until I could barely hold in my laughter. And then we played hangman. It's like a tradition! But this morning, Irma just breezed by as if she barely knew me. She must still be mad from yesterday. But I didn't even do anything!

Hay Lin would have started brooding big-time if Will hadn't interrupted her funk.

"I still don't get what this is about," Will whispered to her friend, gesturing toward the dread-filled faces of the other kids and the auditorium stage, which was packed with big pumpkins.

Hay Lin nodded at Will's confusion. Will hadn't been at Sheffield long enough to know about some of its weirder traditions.

"When I first heard about this day – the great Sheffield Pumpkin Day – I couldn't believe it," she told Will. "It took me three months to believe it wasn't a big joke!"

Martin must have overheard, because he turned around to interrupt Hay Lin's speech.

"Every year," he whispered, "we celebrate the birth of Sherwood J. Sheffield, the founder of the school. It's a tradition."

"Oh," Will said with a shrug. She didn't look impressed. Then she turned back to Hay Lin. "And where are the others? Playing hooky?"

"Cornelia's still at home," Hay Lin said, "Taranee hasn't shown up yet, and Irma's over there."

Hay Lin pointed irritably over at Irma, who was gazing at the stage with a blank expression in her eyes. She wasn't giggling or gossiping, painting her nails, or glossing her lips. She was just . . . *sitting* there.

"What's she doing over there?" Will asked, sounding as bewildered as Hay Lin felt.

"That's what I'd like to know," Hay Lin

huffed. "Last night, I couldn't manage to calm her down, and today, she's avoiding me."

Before Will could reply, Martin twisted back around in his seat. His little eyes gleamed behind the round lenses of his glasses.

"They're starting!" he breathed excitedly. "Let Pumpkin Day begin!"

"Go crazy, Martin," Hay Lin said drily. She shot Irma one last perplexed look before she turned her attention to the auditorium stage.

Ugh, she thought. Without Irma to entertain me, this day is gonna be excruciating.

Mrs. Knickerbocker didn't seem to think so. As she bustled up to the podium on stage, her face broke into a broad smile.

"Over a hundred years ago," she began, "banker Sherwood J. Sheffield decided to donate a school to the city. He personally selected the land on which the building would be built."

Hay Lin sighed. Here we go. Another year, same speech.

Maybe I should offer to spice up the speech for her next year. She liked the Christmas play I wrote. I could add a little humor, maybe a pumpkin-pie recipe or something.

Hay Lin drifted into planning mode, but even planning wasn't enough to escape Mrs. Knickerbocker's loud lecture fully.

"Mr. Sheffield had never been to school himself," Mrs. Knickerbocker was saying, "but he knew that studying was important. He was also a man with a keen sense of humor. He chose a large pumpkin patch to be the grounds, because he loved pumpkins."

Hay Lin couldn't help giggling as she imagined Sherwood J. Sheffield, grinning beneath his moustache as he pointed his walking stick at a field filled with big, orange pumpkins.

"The very first principal of Sheffield Institute, Mr. Folder," Mrs. Knickerbocker continued, "was convinced that Heatherfield's finest minds would grow out of this school the same way the pumpkins grew in the fields. Thus, the pumpkin, and its vines, became the symbol of our school."

No kidding! Hay Lin thought with another quiet laugh. Those pumpkins are everywhere – on the wrought-iron gate that leads to the grounds, over the intercom speaker in every classroom, on every cafeteria tray, even on the tiles in the girls' bathroom!

"Time passed," Mrs. Knickerbocker droned on, "and, seeing the success of the school that bore his name, the elderly Mr. Sheffield donated a vast library to the Institute. This generous gift has continued to grow over Sheffield's one hundred years of existence. And for this, we must thank – "

Here it comes, Hay Lin thought with a grimace. Pumpkin Day's main event.

"We must thank Sherwood Sheffield III," Mrs. Knickerbocker concluded, "the grandson of our beloved founder."

Mrs. Knickerbocker gestured toward the back of the stage, where an extremely old and extremely small man was pulling himself slowly out of his chair. Leaning heavily on a cane, he shuffled up to the podium, waving at the students like an aging celebrity walking a red carpet.

"Hee-hee-heeeeee!" he cackled croakily. He slapped a thick stack of papers onto the podium, and cleared his throat with great fanfare. Then, he began to speak. He spoke of a strange time that he referred to as " . . . back in the old days, when I was a young boy." In fact,

Sherwood J. Sheffield III just talked and talked and talked.

Uggggggh, Hay Lin thought painfully. I'm not sure if I'll make it through this. I need a distraction – please – any distraction!

Desperately, she looked around the front of the auditorium to see what people were doing. All around her, Sheffielders were nodding off, reading books hidden in their laps, or gazing at themselves in compact mirrors.

Hay Lin twisted in her seat to check out the back of the big hall.

Creeeaaaak.

Hay Lin's eyebrows shot up. One of the auditorium doors had just opened, and Taranee's head was peeking through it! Hay Lin glanced at her watch again. It was well after eleven!

Taranee must have *really* overslept, Hay Lin thought. Unless . . . she's late because something's wrong.

Hay Lin squinted to get a reading of Taranee's face. Her friend's glasses were askew on her nose. Her skin looked pale, and her green cardigan was buttoned wrong.

Uh-oh, Hay Lin thought. My hunch was

right. Something's *definitely* wrong.

Hay Lin's muscles tensed. She wanted to jump out of her chair and dash over to her friend to get the scoop.

Unfortunately, Sherwood J. Sheffield III had other ideas. He was still droning on and on.

". . . And I am what I am today thanks to studying, commitment, and hard work," he said. "Which is why inheriting the bank that my grandfather founded certainly came in handy! Thank you for your attention."

With that, Mr. Sheffield did something absolutely shocking. He stopped talking! Mrs. Knickerbocker stepped up to the ancient banker's side with an enormous grin on her face.

"Um, that was a lovely speech, sir," she said.

Mr. Sheffield nodded in avid agreement. The principal turned to the students, who were stretching, rubbing sleep from their eyes, and squirming restlessly.

"Let's say thank you and good-bye to Mr. Sheffield and hope that next year," Mrs. Knickerbocker said enthusiastically, "we can have him on this stage once again."

As the Sheffielders clapped listlessly, the old man assured Knickerbocker, "Oh, I don't know about you, but *I'll* be here."

"Wonderful," Mrs. Knickerbocker said, with a touch of weariness in her voice. "All right students, now let's go out to the entrance hall, where a snack has been prepared – *without running*, please!"

Yeah, right! Hay Lin said to herself as kids all around her shot out of their seats.

"Move, move!" the students cried, pushing their way up the aisles and toward the exits. They surged through the auditorium doors, practically squashing Taranee, who had just made her way into the room. Hay Lin and Will joined the flood of kids rushing to get into the fresh air.

"Will! Hay Lin," Taranee cried, pushing her way over to the two Guardians. "I have to tell you something!"

Will's eyes grew wide, and she shot Hay Lin a guilty glance.

"I have something to tell you, too," she said.

"But my news is important!" Taranee cried.

"Well, so is mine!" Will said heatedly.

"Hey," Hay Lin interjected, trying to keep

everyone calm. "One at a time, guys."

She hoped her voice sounded breezy, because inside, her heart was tense with fear.

And to think *I* actually believed today might be an improvement over yesterday, she thought with a sigh. But it looks like our problems are only getting bigger!

FIVE

Will, Taranee, and Hay Lin finally made their way out of the Sheffield auditorium with the rest of their assembly-weary classmates. The kids milled around on the grass, chattering with one another and angling their faces toward the sun. They were free. They had snacks. They seemed completely happy.

Must be nice to relax and not worry about anything, Will thought.

With a sigh, she turned to face her friends. She didn't know how she could tell them her news.

I still can't quite believe it myself, she thought.

For about the hundredth time that day, it seemed, Will's mind drifted back to the moments leading up to that terrible moment the previous afternoon, when her mother had delivered the dreadful, and totally unfair, news.

As she watched the Sheffielders, Will thought about how she had been in control of her life before her mum had ruined everything with her announcement.

Will had been in Ms. Fix-it mode, a role she'd started to play more and more often since becoming the Keeper of the Heart of Candracar. When a Guardian's feathers were ruffled, Will smoothed them. When the girls were desperate for an idea, Will hatched one. And when a friend's heart ached, Will longed to provide some comfort.

That was why, when she'd stalked away from Cornelia's building the previous day, she'd gone straight to Olsen's Pet Shop. She had an after-school job at the store. She also happened to have a monster crush on Matt Olsen, the owner's grandson. Not only was Matt supercute *and* good with animals, he happened to be the lead singer of Cobalt Blue – one of Will's favorite bands. The job was perfect because Will liked being around the animals and, of course, occasionally seeing dreamy Matt.

But the day before, Will hadn't been scheduled to work, and she hadn't been thinking about how she might catch sight of Matt. No, she'd gone to the store for a totally different reason.

She thought about her visit and smiled.

"Hi, Mr. Olsen," she said in a melancholy tone when she walked through the door. The old, bald parrot perched next to the cash register squawked sadly. A few of the other animals caged in various corners of the shop whimpered and mewed. To be honest, the place sounded downright depressing.

Remembering that she should never enter the pet shop feeling troubled or sad, Will slapped her forehead. Being a Guardian meant not only having superstrength and wings, but having emotions that animals could sense. Which meant that, right away, because Will felt sad, all of the puppies, cats, and hamsters in the store felt depressed, too.

So Will tried to cheer up as she began talking to sweet Mr. Olsen. "I need a very special present," she told him.

"Really?" the old man replied with a grin. "How special are you talking?"

"It's for a good friend who's pretty down," Will said, picturing Cornelia's pale, thin face. "I'd really like to give her something to cheer her up."

"If that's the case," Mr. Olsen said, "then I'd recommend this little guy!"

He knelt to the floor behind the counter. Will peered over his shoulder and grinned – for real this time. Mr. Olsen was fondling the pink ears of a kitten. The kitty's velvety, blue-grey fur was begging to be petted. That is, if you could catch him! The kitten was chasing a ball of yarn around his wicker pet bed, a playful look in his big, green eyes. He was adorable, and Will knew he would put a smile on even Cornelia's pouty face.

"He's really friendly," Mr. Olsen said, giving the kitten's tail a playful tweak. "But he's also very independent and proud for such a little critter."

Independent and proud? Will thought. That sounds just like Cornelia!

Suddenly, the kitten tumbled out of his fluffy bed and scampered over to nuzzle the hem of Will's jeans. Laughing with delight, she scooped the cat up into her arms and giggled as he rubbed her neck.

"I think my friend is going to love him!" Will said, trying to keep the squirming kitten from jumping out of her arms. "She'll take good care of him, too."

"Good to know," Mr. Olsen said kindly. "Well, then, he's all yours."

Will handed the kitten back to the old man and reached into her jeans pocket. She only had ten dollars in allowance money on her. She hoped she'd be able to afford the furry little pick-me-up. "How much do I owe you?" she asked the older man.

Mr. Olsen waved at Will dismissively.

"No charge," he said. "If it's for a sad friend, it's on the house."

"Oh, I couldn't, really!" Will protested.

"But you're going to!" Mr. Olsen declared. He placed the little cat into a wicker carrier and thrust the basket into Will's arms. "Now, run along and take it to her, before I have second thoughts."

"Thanks a million," Will said as Mr. Olsen nudged her through the pet-shop door. "But I'm *going* to pay you back by working at the shop three afternoons next week."

"It's a deal," Mr. Olsen said, giving Will a thumbs-up and a wink.

Will headed back to Cornelia's building. And with every few steps, she giggled as she felt the kitten somersaulting around in the carrier.

I really hope Cornelia likes this present, she thought. It might make talking to her a little easier. There's so much I want to tell her, but I'm not sure I'd manage to put it the right way. Cornelia and I only started seeing eye to eye recently. Before that, she was superskeptical about me.

It makes sense, though, Will mused. Cornelia's a champion figure skater. She's the big sister in her family and she's a total Infielder at school – which is just another way of saying she's cool, popular, pretty, and completely in the know. Then *I* came along. I was new to town. I was totally shy, and yet *I* was the one chosen to lead our save-the-world crew. Cornelia was definitely *not* happy when the Oracle decided I'd be the Keeper of the Heart of Candracar. Cornelia was used to *giving* the orders, not taking them.

It had taken a lot of time – not to mention Will's success in quite a few battles against Cedric and his Metamoorian soldiers – before Cornelia had finally accepted Will's role as leader.

Will suspected that Caleb had also helped Cornelia get over her bruised ego. Meeting him had had a big impact on her. When Cornelia had seen him leading the rebel army that helped restore Elyon to Meridian's throne, she not only fell in love with him, she also learned what really mattered in life: honour, friendship, and teamwork.

In her grief over Caleb's transformation, Will knew, Cornelia had forgotten some of those lessons. Instead, she had spent most of her time alone, ignoring her friends. But who could blame her?

"That's where you come in, kitty," Will said, peeking at the fuzzy little thing through a gap in the wicker carrier's cover. "You're going to keep Cornelia company a lot more than I'll be able to, right?"

The kitten meowed.

A few minutes later, Will arrived at Cornelia's building. The doorman met her at the locked gate. Pushing his cap back to peer into the cat carrier, he said, "Can I help you? I see you've got your hands full."

"Thanks, sir," Will said. "I wanted to drop this off for Cornelia Hale."

"I can take care of that, if you like, miss," the doorman said. "After all, that's what I'm here for."

"That would be really great," Will replied. She knew better than to go up to the Hales' apartment herself. Cornelia probably wasn't in the mood for visitors. But, she couldn't just drop the kitten off with no explanation, though. She wanted Cornelia to know she was there for her and that she understood that Cornelia was feeling lonely. "If it isn't too much to ask," she said to the doorman, "I have a little message for her, too."

As the man nodded amiably, Will dug into her backpack and fished out a scrap of paper and a Magic Marker. She smiled as she scrawled a note.

Will shook her head, emerging from her memories of the previous day. All around her, students were laughing and talking. No one seemed upset or bothered or even the slightest bit lonely. They all seemed happy.

Just like I was when I dropped off the kitten at Cornelia's, Will thought.

She had had no idea that after she left Cornelia's apartment, her mother would ruin the day by announcing that they were moving away from Heatherfield.

Nor could Will have imagined that one day later she'd be standing there staring into the concerned eyes of Taranee and Hay Lin, searching for the words to tell them her horrible news.

No, she couldn't have imagined that turn of events. She'd been filled with confidence as she'd written to Cornelia, in big, bubbly, green letters, "With love, Will."

SIX

Hay Lin looked from Will to Taranee, then back to Will. She couldn't decide which one of them looked more stressed out.

Wow, she thought, feeling her own face get a shade paler. This situation does not look good!

Worriedly, she glanced away and stared for a moment at the students still streaming out of the Sheffield auditorium. One of them was Irma, looking as cold and distant as she had all morning. The sight of her made Hay Lin shift from being upset to being downright annoyed.

I know Irma's stubborn, she told herself, but this is out of *control*. If two of us are in trouble, then we're *all* in trouble, and Irma's not going to worm her way out of hearing about what is going on.

Clenching her fists, Hay Lin turned back to Will and Taranee and declared, "If what you have to say is so important, at least wait until Irma gets here."

The girls nodded, and Hay Lin began to march over to Irma. As she approached her best friend, she formulated a strategy to win her over.

I'll start with a smile, Hay Lin thought, and if she doesn't budge, *then* I'll just have to start playing hardball.

With her plan in place, Hay Lin walked up behind Irma and tweaked one of her friend's honey-brown curls. Irma glanced over her shoulder and looked at Hay Lin with a complete lack of interest.

"Irma?" Hay Lin chirped sweetly. "Could you come here a sec? We're having a special meeting."

"Um," Irma drawled, "could we make it for later, Hay Lin? I've got something to do."

Hay Lin was not going to put up with that attitude. She grabbed Irma's arm.

"Listen," she insisted. "I think that Will and Taranee have a problem."

"I told you," Irma said, continuing to

appear bored, "I've got something to do right now."

Irma shook off Hay Lin's hand and began to wander away into the crowd.

You've got to be kidding me, Hay Lin thought indignantly.

She yelled after Irma, "Don't just walk off when I'm talking to you! What could be more important than your friends?"

Irma paused.

This is it! Hay Lin thought. This is the moment when she totally apologizes, assures me she was just kidding, and rejoins our group.

Irma gazed back at Hay Lin, who continued to smile at her encouragingly.

"Not right now, Hay Lin."

Hay Lin's smile evaporated.

Did I just hear what I think I heard? she sputtered silently. Irma may be in a total funk, but disloyal? Never! What is *up* with –

"Irma!"

Hay Lin jumped. A female voice was beckoning to Irma from in front of the open auditorium doors. The voice was light and giggly. It also, Hay Lin thought, sounded strangely familiar.

"Coming!" Irma called out obediently. She hurried over to where a blue-eyed young woman was leaning against a marble pillar. The teenager's green T-shirt had a low-cut neckline and a high-cut hem. She had way-curvy hips; perfectly waved hair; long, muscular limbs; and a face that, like her voice, seemed strangely familiar.

"Yikes!" Hay Lin suddenly exclaimed. She was just beginning to put two and two together when Will and Taranee hurried over to gaze at the mystery girl standing with Irma. They were just as shocked as Hay Lin was.

"Wh – what on earth is going on?" Will blurted out.

Taranee gulped as she took the scene in.

The only one who wasn't weirded out by the sight of the girl in the green T-shirt was Irma. She smiled up at her and said, "Hi, Stella!"

"Irma, sweetie!" the girl giggled. She cast a sidelong glance at the crowd that was swiftly gathering around her – a crowd that consisted almost entirely of boys.

"I didn't expect to find you here," Stella said, "in the middle of *all* these boys!"

"Seriously, what is going on?" Hay Lin whispered to Will and Taranee. They began pushing through the throng to get closer to Irma and Stella.

They weren't the only ones. As Irma introduced Stella, the boys crowded around. Their eyes glittered, and their smiles looked a bit goofy. They were totally love-struck!

Ewww, Hay Lin thought with a curled lip. They're practically drooling!

And Stella and Irma loved it. They looked happy to lap up all of the attention.

"This is my cousin, Stella!" Irma explained to the boys. "Remember? I told you all about her – and here she is!"

"Uh, hey, Stella!" one of the guys said enthusiastically.

Oh, ick! Hay Lin thought. That's Andrew Hornby. Irma used to have a major crush on him. That is, until she changed into her Guardian self and actually went on a date with him. But when Andrew tried to lay a big, wet smooch on her, Irma turned him into a toad! That was the end of her crush. But clearly this Stella character didn't feel the same way.

"Hi!" the flirty Stella said to Andrew, with a

sly grin. She was acting like she had a crush on Andrew big-time.

The boy ran a hand through his blond hair and took a step closer to Stella.

"Haven't – haven't we met before?" he asked. "Your face – I feel like I've seen you somewhere."

"Who knows!" Stella said with an adorable little shrug. "I go to lots of places and meet lots of people. What's your name?"

Before Andrew could answer, Will thrust herself between the two flirts.

Hey! Hay Lin thought. I didn't see Will sneak over there.

Will was scowling up at the mysterious new visitor.

"*I'll* tell you his name, Stella," she announced boldly. "It's Andrew Hornby. Are you absolutely sure you've never met him before?"

"Huh?" Stella said, confused by Will's tone. Fear flickered in her big, blue eyes. "Er, well . . ."

Will shook her head in frustration. Then she hooked one arm around Stella's, the other around Irma.

"I think it's time for both of you to leave,

now, okay?" she said. "Say good-bye to the boys, Stella!"

Even though Stella was a good head taller than the red-haired Guardian, Will seemed to have no trouble dragging the two "cousins" away from the circle of their admirers. As she quickly walked them toward the school exit, Stella waved over her shoulder.

"Hee-hee," she giggled. "See you around, Andrew."

"You bet," Andrew replied, his eyes wide and focused entirely on her.

Shrugging, Hay Lin and Taranee trailed after the trio. When all of the girls were outside Sheffield's tall, stucco wall, safe from prying eyes, Hay Lin finally spoke.

"Will," she said. "What's got into you?"

"Haven't you figured it out yet, Hay Lin?"

Will was still scowling as she pushed Irma and Stella further along the wall. She looked up accusingly at Stella's beautiful face.

"Why don't you tell them yourself, *Irma*? Or – " Will pointed at the girl Hay Lin knew as Irma. "Or do you want your astral drop to do it for you?"

"Whaaattt?" Hay Lin shrieked.

She looked quickly from the short, round-cheeked girl who resembled her best friend to the girl in the slinky outfit who looked remarkably like another version of her best friend.

Oh. My. God, she thought. *That's* why Stella looked so familiar. No wonder I was so confused. She's Irma, in a magical, grown-up form! The girl who looks like the real Irma is actually a magical double that Irma conjured up.

The guilty look on "Stella's" face gave Hay Lin her confirmation. Irma had transformed herself *and* whipped up an astral drop. She'd totally engaged in abuse of magic.

"I can explain everything!" the real Irma protested, her hands fluttering and waving nervously in front of her.

"There's nothing to explain," Will said, her hands on her hips. "You made an incredibly huge mistake. You transformed yourself to charm Andrew Hornby again! Wasn't turning him into a toad once good enough for you?"

"I wouldn't have hurt anyone, Will," Irma insisted. "It was just a joke."

Yup, Hay Lin thought with a shake of her head. *That's* definitely Irma, all right!

Will wasn't falling for Irma's excuses.

"You're toying with your powers," she said, pointing at Irma accusingly. "And you know that when our last mission ended, the Oracle asked us to use them *wisely*. He said to only use the powers when we actually needed them, and not to just use them for our own amusement. What's got into you? How could you do this?"

"All right, already," Irma cried. "I goofed and I'm sorry. But there's no reason to make such a big deal about it."

Hay Lin followed Irma's gaze as she looked around her. The place was practically deserted. Most of the students had left school already. After that assembly, everyone was thankful to have the rest of the day off. Nobody was nearby, so Irma turned back to Will with a grin.

"Well, at the end of the day, nothing bad happened," she declared.

"I don't agree with you, Irma," Will retorted. "But this isn't the time or place to talk about it. So, make your astral drop disappear, and change back to your own self!" Will did her own scan of the pavement. "Now! Nobody's around."

"Okay," Irma said sheepishly.

Hay Lin watched as Irma closed her eyes and held her hands out before her. Faint wisps of watery blue magic drifted from her fingertips. But Irma's tall and curvy body stayed unchanged.

Irma's eyes snapped open, and her lips formed a surprised *o*.

"Well!" Will demanded. "What are you waiting for?"

"I – I – " Irma stuttered. She stared down at her body. "I can't transform!"

SEVEN

Irma blew a strand of hair out of her long-lashed eyes and glared into the mirror on the wall of Taranee's bedroom. After she had been unable to transform, the four girls had decided to head to Taranee's to figure out a plan. So far, they hadn't come up with any brilliant ideas.

This stinks, Irma thought. I'm a totally beautiful and alluring guy-magnet, and – I'm completely bummed about it! I never thought I would be upset about being more beautiful and mature. But now I want to change back into my old self, and nothing is happening. It's a magic malfunction!

She peeled her gaze from her reflection and reluctantly looked behind her. Will and Hay Lin were glaring at her in disapproval as Taranee bit her lip and peeked anxiously out the window.

"Well?" Will asked Irma testily.

"Well, nothing. Nothing is happening. . . ." Irma complained. She looked down at her body in despair.

"Well, you guys better hurry up," Taranee urged, turning from her post at the window. "My brother could be back any minute now."

"Don't look at me," Hay Lin snapped. "*Irma's* the one who's got to get a move on."

Irma huffed in annoyance, then squeezed her eyes shut and clasped her hands in front of her.

Okay, she said to herself. I don't know if you can hear me up there, Oracle, but if you're trying to teach me a lesson, you've made your point. I promise: Never again will I transform in order to flirt with boys. Not even if the junior prom is coming up and I'm completely dateless. Not even if Andrew Hornby writes a love letter to Stella asking her out and making her (and therefore, me) a shoo-in for junior prom queen. So, please, *pleeeeease*, let me get my old self back. Please.

Nodding with satisfaction, Irma began to

summon up her magic. She wiggled her hands until she felt cool, blue power sparking from her fingertips.

Then she concentrated on one thing and one thing only: transformation.

Transformation, Irma thought, feeling her powers fizz through her limbs. Transformation – transformation – back to my old self again –

Then, Irma felt her magic dissipate. She opened her eyes and looked down.

"N-o-o-o-o-o!" she wailed. She was still "Stella." She turned to Will, who was glaring at her.

"I've been telling you for an hour now," Irma wailed, throwing up her hands in frustration. "It's useless. I can't transform back. My powers aren't working anymore. What – what does all of this mean?"

"I don't know," Will said with a helpless shrug. "Nothing like this has ever happened before."

Oooh, Irma said to herself. This is really bad. This is worse than any punishment even my parents could give me.

Thinking of her parents, Irma tried to picture their reaction to her mature new look. Her dad, a police sergeant with all the gruffness of a bear, would roll his eyes and stomp around the house, muttering about how kids today were growing up way too fast.

And Mum, Irma thought regretfully. She'd get all weepy about missing out on my early teen years, and I'd get a major case of the guilts. Of course, that is, if they lived through the shock of the whole thing.

No, she concluded. I definitely and absolutely can't go home to the parents like this.

"Hey!" Irma said to Will hopefully. "Maybe if you used the Heart of Candracar?"

Will shook her head.

"The Heart of Candracar has nothing to do with it," she said. "We've always managed to change without it."

"Will's right," Hay Lin piped up, plucking a pink hand mirror from Taranee's vanity table. "The Heart just helps us get the most out of our powers."

"Well, that's just great!" Irma shrieked in frustration. "Somebody, do something! I can't stay like this forever!"

"Isn't this what you wanted all along?" Will

shot back, not bothering to hide her anger.

"Oh, give me a break, Will," Irma replied. "This is no time for preaching."

Will crossed her arms over her chest and glared at Irma.

Taranee, however, used her arms to reach out to Irma. She grabbed Irma's grown-up hands in her own girlish ones. Her voice was soft, comforting, and totally wise.

"Concentrate, Irma," she urged her friend. "Don't panic, and think really hard about what you want."

Taranee's voice infused all the girls with a sense of calm ease.

When Will spoke next, her voice had taken on a softer tone. "Taranee's right," she said. "Why don't you try again, Irma?"

Irma balled up her fists and pressed them to her temples. She squinted and focused.

"Yesssss," she hissed. "I swear, if I change back to normal, I'll never do a dumb thing like this ever again!"

"That's the spirit," Will cried. "You can do it. You can do it!"

Irma squeezed her eyes shut and laced her fingers together tightly through her hair.

Changechangechange, she thought desperately. Please, *please*, let me change!

Fzank!

Irma's eyes popped open. Something had happened, all right! She'd heard a horrible sound – like a balloon deflating in a single, sputtery gasp. Her head felt strange.

She glanced at her friends, and all three had the strangest looks on their faces. Taranee had a hand over her mouth. Will had gone pale. And Hay Lin trembled as she held her hand mirror up for Irma to peer into.

When Irma saw her reflection in the trembling mirror, she shrieked.

"I'm hideous!" she cried. "I've got my ordinary head on my Guardian figure! A teensy-tiny head on a huge body. I'm a monster!"

This can't be happening, Irma thought, staring at her distorted self. I can never go to school again! I will have to become a total social outcast. No dating, no hanging out at the mall. I won't even be able to go outside again! Taranee's parents will just have to set up a cot for me in the basement. Maybe throw some leftovers down the stairs every once in a while.

Will's voice broke in upon her thoughts. The

Keeper of the Heart had a different idea. "Keep going," she cried. "You're halfway there, Irma. Give it your best shot!"

Desperately, Irma nodded and squeezed her eyes shut again. She grunted with the effort of summoning more magic.

Fzank!

Hay Lin held up the mirror again.

"Eeep!" Irma cried. Her torso had also switched back to its old appearance – there was just one thing wrong. Actually, two things – and they were fluttering nervously behind her back. She sighed. This was not working out the way she'd planned.

"Now I've got wings!" Irma screeched, peering over her shoulder at the iridescent wings that had just popped through the back of her pink shirt.

"Keep going!" Will called again. "Keep going!"

"Grrrrrrr!" Irma grunted. She pushed and pulled with all her power, throwing every bit of focus she had into her transformation – hoping this time it would actually work.

KZAAAK!

Irma's eyes opened just in time to see a blast of pale blue magic shoot out of her body like a watery explosion. Will's red hair swirled in the magic's wake. She gasped at the impact of her magic, and then she grinned!

Irma looked down at herself.

She saw her favorite old jeans. Her beat-up trainers. Her old, slightly messy hair. She was back to her old self!

"Wow!" Irma breathed. "Am I – am I me again?"

"Sure looks like it," Will gasped. All three girls clustered around Irma. "Welcome back!"

Hay Lin threw her arms around Irma. "Wow!" she cried. "That was freaky. What happened, anyway?"

"That's what I'd like to know," Irma said. Her voice was still shaky after her ordeal. She couldn't wait to relax and recover and –

"Guys?" Taranee said.

Irma looked at her friend. There was no relief in *her* face. In fact, Taranee looked far more worried than she had a few minutes ago.

"Before we figure out Irma's issue," she said. "we've got another problem. I've been trying to tell you about it since this morning – someone might have discovered our secret!"

Oh, great, Irma thought. There goes my rest and relaxation.

"Come take a look," Taranee said. She walked over to her armoire and opened it. On the inside of the door, Irma saw a scrawl in rust-red paint.

I KNOW WHO YOU ARE, the message read.

As Will gasped, Taranee began to pull something out of her back pocket. It was a crumpled photograph. Clutching the photo, she managed to whisper, "Yesterday, there was another message just like this one on the side of my house! No one saw it, luckily. But some-one definitely saw me!"

She handed Hay Lin the photo. Irma crowded in to look at it, too.

It was a photo of Taranee, her glasses off, her eyes shut, her face softened by sleep.

"But this picture – " Hay Lin gasped. "It means that someone must have gotten into your house at night. How creepy."

Taranee looked down and took a deep and shaky breath.

Will stepped over to her and put both hands on her shoulders. "Have you told your folks yet?" she asked, trying to keep her voice from trembling.

"You're the only ones who know," Taranee replied, shaking her head. "I don't know what to do! Maybe I should have warned you before. I'm so scared!"

Taranee walked back to the window and peered through it again. Irma saw her eyes move back and forth, back and forth, scanning the backyard for whoever might be watching her.

Whoa, Irma thought. And I thought being trapped in my Guardian form was a bummer. Imagine being trapped by a stalker!

"Well, one thing's for sure: this does not seem like a joke," Will said.

The four girls stood for a moment in stunned silence, which Irma found to be completely intolerable. Her friends had just talked her out of a very sticky situation. Now it was *her* turn to step up to the plate and take action. She darted over to Taranee and looked into her friend's troubled brown eyes.

"You could sleep over at my place tonight," she offered eagerly.

"That won't solve anything," Will insisted.

"If someone knows our secret, none of us are safe anymore."

"How could this have happened?" Hay Lin wailed. "We were always so careful not to let anyone find out!"

"Well, maybe someone was spying on us," Will proposed. "They might even be watching us this very minute!'

Riiiiiinnnnnggg!

"Aaagh!" Taranee cried, jumping up. The phone next to her bed was ringing. Somehow she knew that there was bad news – or a bad person – on the other end of the line.

Why do I suddenly have the feeling, Irma thought with a deep, sorrowful sigh, that our Guardian vacation is over?

Ri-i-ing!

Irma watched as Taranee walked toward the nightstand, her whole body trembling.

Ri-i-ing!

Taranee slowly reached for the phone. Irma felt as though she were watching a horror movie. Right before she picked it up, she looked at her friends.

Irma saw both terror and guilt behind the lenses of Taranee's glasses. She shook her head. She knew Taranee was too freaked to read her thoughts with her telepathic powers. But she sent her an encouraging message, anyway.

We'll stick with you, Taranee, she thought. *Through anything!*

To herself, Irma added, I just hope that "anything" isn't too horrible! But, I guess we'll find out soon enough.

Ri-i-i-i-i-i-innnngggg!

EIGHT

As the phone on her nightstand rang, Taranee toyed with the idea of just not answering it.

Ignorance is bliss, right? she thought. Maybe I'd rather *not* know who's watching me.

She felt like a little kid again, scared of the monsters in the closet.

The only difference was that, back when she was a little girl, the monster had been imaginary, Taranee thought. Now there really could have been a monster! Or at least, an enemy.

She hesitantly reached for the phone.

"Go on, Taranee," Will whispered encouragingly. "Answer it."

Taranee looked over at her friend with wide eyes and picked up the phone.

"Hello?" she said in a quavering voice.

After a long pause, a voice on the other end spoke up. "Hello, Taranee."

Taranee froze. The voice belonged to a man. It was deep and throaty, with a harsh, taunting edge. The sound of that voice uttering her own name was absolutely chilling.

"Wh – who is this?" Taranee asked.

"Oh, you don't know me," the voice crooned menacingly. "But I know who you are!"

"What do you want from me?" Taranee asked. She was gripping the phone so tightly her knuckles burned. But there was no way she could unclench her fingers. She was too terrified. "Why don't you leave me alone?" Taranee wailed.

"Because," the voice replied calmly. "You owe me a favor. Well, me – and your brother Peter."

At the sound of her brother's name, Taranee felt as though she'd been kicked right in the stomach.

"Peter?" she whispered. "What does Peter have to do with this? What are you talking about?"

"You'll find out soon enough," the man said. His voice was crisp and businesslike. "I'll be waiting for you in half an hour at the Heatherdome Mall."

Taranee had a million questions for this stranger, but they all lay strangled in her throat. Luckily, the man went on.

"Your brother is fine," he explained. "If you do what I tell you, he'll be going home tonight. So here's the deal: don't bring your friends along. Don't show up transformed. And don't try pulling one of your 'cloning' tricks or anything like that."

Panicked tears began spilling out of Taranee's eyes. This guy wasn't bluffing! He really did know all about Taranee. He knew she had the ability to transform. And he knew she had a knack for conjuring up an astral drop, or clone, that could take her place – and take the fall – if she ever ran into trouble.

Perhaps he could even read Taranee's mind, because his next sentence voiced exactly what she'd just been thinking.

"As I told you before," he declared, "I really do know who you are."

"B – but I don't know who you are," Taranee squeaked. "How will I recognise you?"

"In half an hour, you'll find out."

Click!

The dial tone began droning in Taranee's ear. She was so stunned she could barely put the receiver back in its cradle. As soon as she did, she buried her face in her hands. Feeling the steady pressure of Will's hand on her back, Taranee could only wail, "He . . . he's got Peter! He's got *Peter!*"

Twenty-five minutes later, the group stumbled off a city bus in front of the Heatherdome Mall. Taranee gazed up at the blimp-shaped building and felt a mixture of despair and rage. Other girls were in the mall sampling lipstick at department stores or flirting with boys in the food court.

Taranee, on the other hand, was there to meet an evil stranger: her brother's kidnapper.

"Well, here we are," Taranee rasped. She glanced at her watch. "Only five minutes before I'm supposed to meet him."

Will gazed at her, her brown eyes clouded with concern. "So, you'll stick to our plan?" she asked.

Taranee nodded weakly.

"We'll wait out here," Will assured her, "so we won't be noticed."

"And I'll keep in touch with you telepathi-cally," Taranee agreed. "Okay."

Irma flashed one of her trademark grins.

"Don't be nervous!" she chirped. "If any-thing happens, we'll be there in a flash."

"You'll see, Taranee," Hay Lin added with a vigorous nod of her blue-black pigtails. "Everything's going to be just fine."

"Y – yeah," Taranee stammered. "Of course it will."

But as she stepped onto the escalator that led up to the Heatherdome's central atrium, she felt anything but confident. She felt only fearful and lonely. As she scanned the crowd flooding into the mall, every man she saw looked as though he could have been the guy – like that man with the goatee and crabby scowl, or that one with the broad shoulders and greasy hair.

But neither of those guys gave her a second glance.

Taranee looked expectantly at another man with a long ponytail, but he passed her by.

Taranee almost sobbed. Where was he?

She looked at her watch again. It was three-thirty, on the dot.

I hope I don't have to wait too much longer, Taranee thought with a sigh.

She meandered over to a glass partition behind which was a fountain. In the thick, greenish glass, she could see her reflection. Her face looked drawn. Her shoulders were slumped. She looked weak and small – especially in comparison to the very tall figure who had just walked up behind her!

Taranee froze. Without turning around, she gazed at the man's reflection in the glass. He wore a long grey trench coat over a black turtle-neck, and his head was shaved so close it shone. He glared down at Taranee with deep-set, brooding eyes.

"Hello, Taranee."

Taranee gulped. Trembling visibly, she turned to face the sinister stranger.

"Why don't we sit down over there and have a little chat?" the man said casually.

"O – okay," Taranee stuttered.

The man clamped a hand on her shoulder and led her to a nearby bench. Taranee tried to stave off her growing panic by following the plan she and her friends had made.

Okay, I'm with the stalker, she told herself.

Now, I have to contact Will telepathically.

Taranee touched her fingers to her temple and concentrated. She focused all her mental energy on forming a bridge of communication between her and her best friend. She'd talked to Will telepathically dozens of times before. The connection started with Taranee's vision going blurry; then she found her friends in her mind.

As she prepared to make the connection now, her vision went blurry as usual.

But she couldn't make contact!

Taranee's eyes went wide with terror.

Wh – what's happening to me? she screamed inside her head. *My telepathic powers – they've disappeared!*

Taranee could picture what her friends would be doing now, as they waited for her message – a message that would never come.

Irma would be gazing at the big mall clock and tapping her foot. "It's a quarter past four," she'd be saying impatiently. "Why hasn't Taranee contacted us yet?"

"Maybe the guy didn't show," Hay Lin, ever the optimist, would propose. "You're not the only one who can be late."

Irma would shake her head and start stomping toward the Heatherdome Mall.

"This is the kind of appointment where you show up right on time," she'd insist. "I think we should go take a look."

Taranee sighed. She knew exactly what Will's reaction would be to such a proposal.

"No," she'd declare, pulling Irma back by the elbow. "Let's wait a little longer."

If only Will knew that her sensible leadership is way off base this time, Taranee thought.

Speaking of which, Taranee had to get back to the matter at hand. The man was now shoving her onto the bench and sitting down next to her.

Taranee forced herself to start asking questions. Without information, she could not defend herself.

"Who are you?" she asked, trying to keep the squeak out of her voice. "I've never seen you before."

"I'm a Guardian-hunter, Taranee," the man growled. "And so far, I've found four of you! I'm missing just one – the one with the long, blond hair."

Taranee felt her heart begin to thump hard

in her chest. Will had been right. *All* of the Guardians were in danger.

"B – but why are you doing this?" Taranee demanded. "What exactly do you want from us?"

"I want just one thing, little lady," the man said with an evil, yellow-toothed grin. "To destroy you!"

Taranee almost burst into tears. But another part of her – the strong, brave, Guardian side – wouldn't allow that to happen.

"You still haven't answered my question," Taranee told the man, refusing to acknowledge his threat.

"If you do what I ask of you," the man responded, "Peter will go back home safe and sound, without remembering anything that happened to him."

I have a pretty good feeling that this guy is not going to ask me to do anything easy, Taranee thought. She felt annoyance growing in the pit of her stomach.

"Why do you hate us so much?" she asked the stranger. "What did we ever do to you?"

"You want an answer, Taranee?" the man asked slyly. Suddenly, he waved his hand before his face.

Zwiiinng!

With a shimmer of magic, the man was transformed. His pale, shining skin became leathery and cobalt blue. His bald head immediately sprouted a mop of yellow hair. His teeth grew into large fangs, and his small, human ears turned into the pointy ears of a Metamoorian creature.

And not just *any* creature. Taranee knew this guy!

"You!" she gasped.

"Is this enough of an explanation?" the creature asked.

"You – you're Frost," Taranee said. Even the mere mention of the name of Phobos's ruthless hunter made her shudder. The first time she'd gone to Metamoor, Frost had grabbed her and thrown her into a tower, where the evil prince had manipulated her into doubting her friends.

Which basically makes Frost, Taranee thought with a gulp, my worst nightmare!

Without thinking, she jumped off the bench, trying to get as far away as she could from the nasty Metamoorian.

"What are you doing in Heatherfield?" she choked.

"Sit down," Frost barked. In his nonhuman form, his voice was even more gravelly and sinister than it had been before his transformation. "I'm here to settle a score with you."

Knowing her brother's life was at stake, Taranee came over and sank reluctantly back down onto the bench. Frost explained, "You and your friends are responsible for the downfall of Prince Phobos and for the revolt in Meridian. Now, you're going to pay for it."

As Taranee suppressed a shiver, Frost went on with his explanation.

"Tracking you down was child's play," he said. "I learned your distinct psychic prints the day I captured you. Your inner thoughts left me a trail."

This time, Taranee couldn't hide her shivers. She didn't like to think about that day – about the feel of Frost's cold fingers clamped around her arms, about the loneliness of watching her friends escape without her.

Frost, luckily, was oblivious to Taranee's distress. He was too absorbed in his self-congratulatory explanation.

"I followed you," he crowed. "I saw your house, your family; and I discovered your secret!" He paused. His menacing blue face grew thoughtful for a moment. "I have to admit, I didn't recognise you at first in your normal clothes and appearance. But then today, outside the school, I understood everything. You can transform! But this time, you won't save yourself."

With a sharp *thwap*, Frost transformed himself back into the human body he'd conjured up. Taranee could still see hints of the hunter's crooked nose and blocky jaw even in his human form.

"And now," Frost continued, "thanks to you, I'm also going to find your other friend. You're going to take me to her! Let's get going."

Clasping Taranee's shoulder, Frost dragged her to her feet. She struggled in his grasp until Frost bent over to hiss in her ear. "Before you try to run away or ask for help, remember your brother," he warned.

Taranee turned from Frost in defiance. But inside, she was desperate.

My only chance now is to warn Will and the others, she thought.

She began to concentrate so hard she could

feel the blood pounding in her head. Silently, she shouted out to her friends.

Can you hear me? she screamed in her mind. *We have to stop this monster! We have to save Peter! We have to help Cornelia. Help! Help! Hellllllllp!*

NINE

Frost grinned as he pulled Taranee along through the crowded mall. He was very pleased that his plan to capture the Guardians was finally beginning to come together. He had waited too long for this moment. His journey had been long, and he had been very patient.

As he walked with Taranee through the mob of shoppers, he thought about how his adventure in Heatherfield had begun. His thoughts turned to a recent day, when he had been convinced that he would never find the Guardians. He smiled as he remembered pacing in front of the large, pink building that housed the Sheffield Institute.

It was early afternoon and he was getting

fed up with waiting around.

Frost watched as the humans passing him on the pavement laughed and chatted under the bright sun. He did not like Heatherfield and the strange habits of humans. Plus, the top of his hairless head was beginning to burn.

But the sunburn was nothing compared to the irritation forming *inside* his head.

Frost was irritated by many things. He loathed cheerful, sunny days like this one. He despised happy people. Most of all, he didn't like it when prey eluded him. And that was exactly what he was contending with as he paced outside the pink building. Wrapping his long, grey trench coat more tightly around him, Frost leaned against a tree trunk to ponder his problem.

At the beginning, everything had made sense – when Phobos ruled over Metamoor with brilliant cruelty. My lord, the prince, never would have allowed a sun-drenched day like this to happen, he thought. He controlled the weather as easily as he controlled the people. Metamoorian sunshine was for Phobos and Phobos only.

Once, *I* was for Phobos only, too, Frost

thought with an angry grunt. I was the prince's prize hunter, and nobody was safe from my claws. A peasant who'd said disparaging things about our ruler in the marketplace, or a thief who'd threatened to steal from Phobos? I could pluck him out of the streets and toss him into prison before he knew what had happened.

I could bring down a stag with my bare hands and then serve it to Phobos at a royal banquet later that day.

I was a menace to all who invaded the city of Meridian, Frost thought with a grin.

Then Elyon returned to Metamoor and everything began to change, Frost thought, his face returning to its usual scowl. Not only had that blond-haired brat wanted to snatch the throne away from Prince Phobos, she had also had some meddlesome friends – the Guardians of the Veil. The girls had trailed Elyon to Meridian and wrought havoc in the city. They had used their magic to infiltrate the city's secret underground and even managed to sneak into Phobos's forbidden garden, evading the thicket of poisonous black roses that protected it like barbed wire.

Phobos had put his thick-necked soldiers

on the case, sending them out to capture the intruders, Frost recalled. When those soldiers proved themselves to be incompetent, the prince had called in his star sleuth – Frost! With his fire-breathing steed and his incomparable tracking skills, Frost was supposed to be impossible to shake.

Except, somehow, the Guardians *had* shaken him. They'd slipped through his claws by tricking him into capturing their astral drops instead of their real selves.

Another time, they'd humiliated him by luring him through a church door that was too short for his large frame. He'd bashed his head into the doorjamb and passed out. To make it even more embarrassing, all of this had taken place in front of an entire crowd of peasants who were all booing Frost.

The Guardians had put an end to Frost's impeccable string of captures, and then they had done something far, far worse.

They had conquered Phobos.

Meridian's prince and his sidekick, Cedric, were languishing in the Tower of Mists now. They had been made prisoners of the Oracle of Candracar by those infernal Guardians.

Frost craved revenge. Retribution. A strike back, on behalf of his master.

"When Phobos's imprisonment is over," Frost growled under his breath, "as will surely happen one day, he will be pleased to find that I have disposed of his enemy. Very pleased, indeed."

First, Frost had to find out where the enemy was hiding. But now, as he waited in the shadows, his hunting skills were failing him once again.

It doesn't make sense! Frost railed silently. I'm certain the Guardians live in Heatherfield. All clues point to that. But when I traced their psychic prints to their homes, the Guardians were nowhere to be found. All I found was a group of girls. Those girls, in blue jeans and sweaters, were much too young and ordinary to be the Guardians.

But still, Frost thought, there was something about them that piqued my interest. That was why I followed one – the shy, bespectacled one, Taranee. She reacted to my little messages with absolute panic. Then, I managed to tail her when she dashed to this large building brimming with scampering youths. The sign said it was the so-called Sheffield Institute, which I figured was where Taranee goes to school. But this Sheffield has so far given me no more clues to the Guardians' whereabouts.

"Yaaayyyy!"

Frost's thoughts were suddenly interrupted by a joyful shout emitted by what sounded like at least a dozen young voices. Snorting in disgust, the hunter turned to one of the doors in the pink building. It had been thrown open, and children were spilling through it.

So many kids, Frost scoffed. There's clearly not a Guardian in this crowd. I'm wasting my time here.

But then, Frost stopped grumbling and stood still.

In the middle of the throng of kids, Frost had just spotted a youngster who stood out from the crowd.

Youngster, actually, wasn't a fair description of the girl. Her sparkly eyes and smiling mouth were clearly perceived as beautiful by the admirers surrounding her.

At least one young girl in the crowd – a scrawny thing with a thatch of red hair – seemed to agree with Frost. She stormed over to the beauty and grabbed her by the elbow. Then she grabbed another student – a short girl with a guilty look in her eyes. The redheaded spitfire then proceeded to drag both of her captives out of the school yard.

To Frost's shock, his prey, the girl known as Taranee, followed. Walking along with her was another girl – a tiny thing with almond-shaped eyes and glossy black hair.

The group convened outside the wall that enclosed the school grounds.

Frost gave the girls a piercing glare.

Why, he thought in rage, has my hunt taken me in this strange direction?

As the hunter complained silently to himself, his beady eyes drifted to the oldest-looking girl in the group. The tall one in the tight green sweater. It looked as though she was getting into some kind of trouble.

Now the girl in green was turning around. She seemed to be scanning the area to make sure nobody was spying on her. Frost ducked behind the stucco wall and peeked out, just in time to get a good look at the girl's face. What he saw made him gasp.

The girl looked exactly like one of the

Guardians he'd seen in Metamoor!

Frost's breath quickened as he tried to listen to the redhead's words.

"You *transformed* to try to charm Andrew Hornby again?" she railed.

Transformed, eh? Frost thought, as he looked down at his own human hands and raised his eyebrows. Now I understand. *These* girls are the meddlers I was looking for – the Guardians. It's just that only one of them has transformed!

Frost almost laughed out loud.

Now that I've found my prey, he thought triumphantly, nothing will stop me from taking my revenge!

Frost felt his mouth watering. He had four of the five Guardians right at his fingertips. He wanted nothing more than to jump out and capture the girls then and there. However, one problem remained.

Four of the Guardians was not enough, he told himself. He needed the fifth as well – the one with the long yellow hair, the sour scowl, and the power over earth.

Yes, Frost thought. I want *all* of the Guardians to suffer just as Prince Phobos has suffered. And I know just how to make that happen. I've already invaded Taranee's home. Now, I'll start in on her family!

In the end, it wasn't difficult.

Frost pondered the information he'd gathered from observing Taranee's sleek, white house. He thought of all the family members, then carefully chose his prey – the boy. He'll be the easiest one, Frost thought with a devious smile. He's unsuspecting and nice – qualities that, once I get through with him, he'll soon learn to regret having.

With that decision made, Frost merely had to lurk among the hedges on the corner of Taranee's street until his target appeared. The boy walked with long-legged strides, a basket-ball propped easily under one arm. His hair was woven into ropey twists and he sported a goatee. A pleasant half-smile was on his face and Frost could swear the boy was humming to himself.

Peter L. Cook, Frost thought. The *L*, I know, stands for Lancelot. But, if Taranee doesn't cooperate with me, the *L* will stand for *lost*!

It was time for Frost to make his move. Planting an expression on his human face that was a combination of kind and worried, he stepped out from the hedges.

"Hello, there," Frost called out to the boy.

"Huh?" Peter replied, stumbling to a halt and turning around to face the stranger. Frost had clearly caught Peter off guard.

"Excuse me," Frost said, careful to keep the deep, unfriendly growl out of his voice. "I am sorry to bother you, but could I ask you a favor?"

"Sure," Peter said. His eyes were a bit wary, but he walked toward the hulking, bald man anyway.

"I'm having some car problems back there," Frost said, waving vaguely toward a nearby alley. "If you could give me a push, maybe I'll be able to start her up."

Inwardly, Frost snickered, pleased with his cleverness. While he'd paced outside of Taranee's school, he had eavesdropped on several human conversations. He'd learned that the smelly, gasoline-powered carts the humans drove were called cars. Frost learned from the conversations that the cars also seemed to be constantly coughing, making wretched grinding noises, and refusing to start.

"Dead battery, huh?" Peter said. His face melted into a sympathetic smile. "I hear ya. Okay. Let's go."

Frost leered and turned to lead Peter into the alley. The hunter's jaw was clenched and he sensed that his eyes were glowing red. He kept his back to the boy as they walked. He couldn't risk giving away his true identity – yet.

Only when the pair was out of sight of all human eyes, did Frost turn around. Peter was glancing about the narrow and empty lane in confusion.

"But, wait," Peter sputtered. "Where's the car?"

Frost opened his mouth, letting his full growl rumble out like an uncaged beast.

"There is no car!" he yelled at Peter, "but that doesn't necessarily mean you'll be leaving on foot."

The boy barely had time to react before Frost had made his strike.

He swooped across the alley, his trench coat fluttering behind him. Nothing could come between him and his prey now. He enclosed the boy in his arms and placed his finger on a pressure point just behind Peter's ear. Instantly,

Peter slumped over, unconscious.

Throwing the boy's slack body over his shoulder, Frost skimmed out of the alley. Keeping an eye out for any stray observers that could give him trouble, he began to hurry to his next destination: a dank, cement cavern in an abandoned factory.

Once he'd dragged the boy's limp body down the stairs, Frost used magic to conjure up his favorite kind of restraint: a Stunning Orb. He placed the giant, gaseous sphere in the center of the room, a good ten feet above the hard cement floor.

Satisfied with the roiling Stunning Orb, Frost heaved the boy off the floor and tossed him into the giant ball. Peter penetrated its surface with a crackling sound. In a few seconds, the orb did its magic and the boy's body rolled over in a dead man's float in the center of the circle.

"I hope you don't get too bored while I'm out," Frost called up to the floating figure. "You'll be safe and sound in here, and when I get back, I'll bring along someone to keep you company!"

Yes, Frost thought, yesterday was a good day. And as he grasped Taranee's shoulder with his human hand, he knew that now his days in Heatherfield were going to go just as he had planned.

TEN

Hay Lin was not usually a pessimistic person. Where other people saw an annoying rain shower, she saw potential flowers. A rip in the seat of her jeans? Just an opportunity for a cool, new, funky patch.

But as she, Will, and Irma waited for a message from Taranee – and kept waiting – Hay Lin started to get a little worried.

When the glaring silence in the girls' minds went on a few minutes more, Hay Lin's worry began to grow into full-blown anxiety.

By the fifteen-minute mark, Hay Lin was petrified.

We're *never* going to hear from Taranee, she thought, wringing her hands in despair. Where *is* she? What if this horrible stalker has kidnapped her, just like Peter? Maybe he's scaring her. Or –

HELP!

Hay Lin cringed and clapped her hands to her ears. A scream had suddenly echoed through her mind. It was so loud and shrill that it brought tears to her eyes. She felt herself pale at the pain, and then she took a deep breath to try and calm herself.

Opening her eyes a moment later, Hay Lin saw that Irma and Will were wincing as well.

And the screams weren't stopping.

Help, Cornelia!

"Aaagh!" Will gasped.

– nelia!

"Aaargh!" Irma groaned.

CORNELIA!

"Yikes!" Hay Lin shrieked. Just when she thought she couldn't take any more, the shouting stopped. With sighs of relief, the three girls straightened up and tried to shake the pounding pain from their heads. Finally, Will found the strength to speak.

"Did you hear that?" she asked her friends breathlessly. "It was definitely Taranee!"

"It was like some sort of a mental scream,"

Irma said, her eyes widening in shock. "Maybe she's in danger."

Hay Lin was nodding when something caught her eye. In her peripheral vision, she saw a moss-green sweater and a long, beaded braid glinting in the sun.

Hay Lin turned and pointed urgently. It was Taranee! She was a couple of hundred yards away and walking fast.

And why was she walking *away* from her friends? Because she was being shoved along by a very tall, very muscular, and very evil-looking bald man in a long grey trench coat.

"Forget *maybe,* Irma," Hay Lin shrieked, pointing to Taranee's retreating figure. "Take a look over there!"

Will and Irma followed Hay Lin's gaze.

"Who is that big ape?" Irma squeaked when she saw who Hay Lin had been looking at. Without waiting for an answer, she clenched her fists and cried, "Let's follow them!"

"Yeah, but not like this," Will said. "We can't let that guy see us!"

Hay Lin threw her hands above her head and summoned up her magic. Wind whooshed around her like a cool, tingly breeze. "No sweat," she declared to her friends. "They can't see us if we're invisible!" The burst of air ruffled her long hair, rustled her short skirt, and made her feel as buoyant as a bird. The sensation of power that coursed through her made her heart beat faster.

When the feeling finally subsided, Hay Lin looked down at herself and saw only a faint outline. To everyone but her fellow Guardians, it would have appeared as though she had disappeared into thin air. Unfortunately, her friends didn't seem nearly as delighted by that development as Hay Lin was.

"What are you doing?" Irma demanded. "Somebody could have seen you!"

"Still spooked after your little transformation snafu?" Hay Lin laughed. "Well, don't worry. Nobody saw that except you two."

Hay Lin started walking toward the street. Taranee and the big lug had just crossed to the other side. The other girls didn't have a moment to lose.

As Hay Lin stepped off the curb and onto the crosswalk, she looked back at Irma and Will, who were hurrying after her. They might not approve of her disappearing act, but at least they weren't ditching her.

"If I'm invisible," she declared, "I can stay right on the trail without that guy noticing."

Hay Lin thought her plan was brilliant. So she was surprised to see Will's face contorted in a grimace of horror.

"Oh, no!" her friend cried.

What's her problem? Hay Lin thought. Even if Will doesn't *love* my idea, it's *not* that bad. She shot Will a hurt glare as she continued to cross the street.

That's when Will charged toward her.

"Look out, Hay Lin!" she screamed.

Hay Lin gasped as Will tackled her. It was only when the two girls landed in a heap on the street's opposite curb that she noticed a truck barreling by. All the breath flew out of Hay Lin's lungs as she realised what had almost happened. If Will hadn't shoved her out of the way, that truck would have mowed her down! Because Hay Lin was invisible, as far as the truck driver knew, there had been nobody in his path.

The driver screeched to a halt and hopped out of the driver's seat. He ran over to Will, yelling, "Hey! You okay? Why did you throw yourself in front of my truck!"

Will was still bleary from her fall, and Hay Lin, of course, couldn't say a word. So Irma rushed over. Sporting a big grin, she explained to the driver, "Everything's fine. My friend's just a bit weird. She loves crossing the road with some flair!"

A curious crowd was gathering.

Uh-oh, Hay Lin thought. Irma's got an audience. Now the performance is really going to begin!

"She's an original type, you know," Irma told the onlookers, pointing at Will with an indulgent smile.

Will, meanwhile, was dealing with Hay Lin. Grabbing her by an invisible shoulder, she hissed, "The next time you decide to disappear, try not to do it in the middle of traffic!"

"Uh," Irma suddenly piped up to the crowd, which was beginning to look very confused. "Yeah, she's an odd one, all right. Every once in a while, she even talks to herself."

Some in the group shrugged, and the crowd dispersed. A minute later, the three Guardians were alone again. Irma wiped her brow dramatically and hurried over to where Will and Hay Lin were standing.

"Good going, Hay Lin," she scolded. "That was a close call. And thanks to your brilliant idea, we also lost track of Taranee!"

Hay Lin gasped and looked all around. Irma was right. Taranee was gone!

"I – I didn't mean to!" Hay Lin gulped. "I'm really sorry."

Irma rolled her eyes.

"Forget the apologies and just turn visible again," she said matter-of-factly. Irma was in no mood to joke around. "We may still have time to catch up with the two of them."

Nodding, Hay Lin clenched her fists and waited for the supernatural, fizzy feeling to fill her limbs. She waited for the cool whoosh of air, for the sparkles of silvery magic, for the strong surge of power.

She waited and she waited. But when a moment later she was still invisible, she gasped and looked toward her friends in horror. This couldn't be happening!

"I'm trying, but it isn't working!" she shrieked. "I'm still see-through!"

"What's happening to us?" Irma cried.

"I don't know," Hay Lin wailed. "All I know is, I really don't want to stay invisible."

Will clutched at Hay Lin's ghostly hand.

"Keep calm," she told her. "It happened to Irma, too. Maybe it's only a temporary thing. We'll solve this, too, okay? Just don't panic."

"O – kay," Hay Lin said in a choked voice.

But she wasn't sure she really meant it. She found it hard to breathe as she trooped behind her friends in pursuit of Taranee, completely invisible.

When Irma spoke up, she sounded just as shaken as Hay Lin felt.

"We have to catch up with Taranee," she said urgently. "But how?"

"We've only got one lead," Will said with a pained shrug. "In her telepathic message, Taranee said something about Cornelia. Whatever she meant by that, that's where we're going!"

Normally, Hay Lin was assured by Will's decisive leadership. But now, as she followed the redheaded leader to Cornelia's building – a place where they were certainly not welcome at the moment – she felt as if her optimism had checked out permanently. With her powers all wacky and the group split up, she was feeling definitely down.

I have this horrible feeling, she thought. First, the Power of Five goes on the fritz. Then, my magical powers go AWOL. Everything I could count on a few days ago is disappearing – including me!

ELEVEN

Cornelia grumbled as she flipped over another page in her notebook. After missing school for several days, she had piles of homework to do. And her little sister's scampering around her room squeaking and squawking wasn't helping matters at all.

"Come on, Napoleon!" Lilian piped from under the bed. "Get the ball, like a good kitty!"

Napoleon, Cornelia thought. What a dumb name for a cat. Come to think of it, the whole idea of that cat is dumb! What on earth had Will been thinking?

Cornelia had barely been able to look at the little blue-grey fluff-ball since her doorman had plopped the cat's basket onto her foyer floor yesterday. Even worse, the doorman handed her a note, and then had the nerve to tip his hat and saunter back to the elevator, whistling annoyingly.

The contents of the note had been even more irksome than the cat was.

"With love, Will," the green scrawl on the note had read.

Cornelia had glared at the kitten. He was curled up peacefully behind the bars of his carrier door. His big, round eyes seemed to smile up at her and he purred contentedly.

Why is *everyone* in such a good mood today? Cornelia had thought with a deep sigh. What is there to feel good about? That's what I want to know.

"So, now what am I going to do with you?" she had asked the cat with a sniff.

At that moment, Lilian had popped around the corner and happily skipped into the front hallway.

Lilian had a nose for business that was not her own. But in this case, that wasn't such a bad thing.

"Can I keep the kitty?" Lilian had squealed, darting across the floor and sliding next to the cat's basket. "He's cute!"

"Perfect," Cornelia had said mirthlessly. "He's all yours, Lilian."

Cornelia had then turned and headed for the stairs. She couldn't wait to get back to her room and slam the door. She wanted to forget about everyone – her sister, Will, that silly little cat, *everyone*! Well, everyone except for one person.

Caleb.

Once again, the thought of her lost love's name made the image of his face suddenly appear in Cornelia's mind. Vividly, she saw his strong jaw, the green stripes on his cheeks, the dark, angry eyes that had melted every time he'd laid eyes upon Cornelia.

She smiled a little. Picturing Caleb always put a smile on her face – at least for a little while.

As Cornelia climbed the next step up to her room, the image in her mind had suddenly changed. Caleb's beautiful eyes went vacant. Then, his eyelids blended into his cheeks and forehead, disappearing altogether. His face dissolved into a featureless, white plane. The green stripes on his cheeks curled and expanded until they became dewy, emerald-colored leaves. The white blank that was Caleb's face became a flower petal. Before her eyes, Caleb became a blossom.

It was the flower that sat alive but inert in a basin of water on Cornelia's desk. It was this very flower that occupied her mind and heart constantly.

Cornelia felt a familiar stab of grief in her chest. It took her breath away and made her eyes blur.

In the living room, Lilian was giggling and carrying the kitten in her arms. Cornelia was happy to have both the pet and the sister out of her hair.

But no, Lilian wasn't going to let her get away that easily.

As Cornelia hit the top step of the staircase – seconds away from a clean getaway – Lilian had yelled a question at her back.

"Can I call him Napoleon?" her sister squeaked.

Cornelia didn't even bother turning around. She hadn't wanted Lilian or their mother – who was sitting on the living-room couch sipping a cup of tea – to see her tearstained face. She didn't feel like explaining herself. So she'd merely tossed her answer coldly over her shoulder.

"Like I said, Lilian, he's all yours."

Lilian had clapped her hands in delight and shouted out, "My Napoleon!" as Cornelia had locked herself back in her room.

Now, a day later, her funk was still going strong, and Lilian and Napoleon's antics under her bed were making it worse. Since Cornelia was sprawled on her stomach on top of the bed doing her homework, Lilian could not have chosen a worse playground. Every move she made, made Cornelia more annoyed.

"Come on, kitty!" the younger girl was chirping. Her little head bumped up against the bottom of Cornelia's mattress as she romped with her new pet.

"Let's try again," Lilian squeaked. "Get the ball!"

Bump! Thump! Whump!

"Please, Lilian!" Cornelia finally shouted a little louder than she probably should have.

Lilian's rosy-cheeked face looked out from under the bed and peered up at Cornelia curiously.

"I already asked you before!" Cornelia scowled. "Why can't you and your new cat friend go play somewhere else?"

"But he likes to play here!" Lilian said. To prove her point, she tossed the yellow ball to the floor. Napoleon leaped out from beneath the bed and pounced on the thing, batting it around with his tiny paws.

"I don't care if he likes it in here!" Cornelia yelled. Overcome with frustration, she threw her notebook off the bed. It slammed into the wall with a satisfying *thwap*, then fell to the floor.

"I don't want that animal in my sight," Cornelia shouted. "Get out of my room. NOW!"

Only when Cornelia's voice reached maximum volume did Lilian finally get it. Sticking her tongue out at her big sister, she scooped the kitten up and slung him over her shoulder like a baby doll.

"Come on, Napoleon," she huffed with an exaggerated sigh. "We're not welcome here."

Lilian stalked out of the room as fast her legs could carry her. From his perch on the little girl's shoulder, Napoleon shot Cornelia a sad look. Then he glanced at the bloom on Cornelia's desk and emitted a long, pathetic meow.

It was the saddest sound that Cornelia had ever heard – and it only managed to make her even angrier.

"Why doesn't Will just take that cat back?" she thought with a resentful sniff. "Nobody wants it, and nobody asked her for it in the first place! She wanted to do something nice, thinking she could cheer me up with a *pet*. Ridiculous! I don't want consolation from anybody. I don't want anything except to be left alone, for as long as I feel like it."

Alone.

Cornelia gazed over at her desk. The glowing white lily placed carefully in the center of her desk seemed to pulsate with life. She could feel Caleb's presence in the room.

Yet, at the same time, she was utterly, abysmally alone.

And the truth was, even if she acted like it, she *didn't* feel like being by herself. She missed get-togethers with her friends. She missed sauntering down the halls of the Sheffield Institute, chatting and gossiping.

She missed being happy.

She missed being a not-heartbroken girl.

She missed her best friend, Elyon.

As for Will and Taranee and the others? Well, Cornelia missed them, too, but now she also sort of resented them.

Just then, it seemed to Cornelia that Irma and Hay Lin were superclose, and that Will and Taranee were always together. They made up a neat little foursome.

The only one who's left out in this formula, Cornelia thought bitterly, is me! My true love has become a flower, and my best friend is queen of a distant world. I have nobody. It's so unfair!

Cornelia sank deeper down onto her bed's fluffy comforter, feeling weighed down by her grief. She felt as if she were caught in a black cloud – a thick, choking fog that nothing could permeate.

"Cornelia!"

Nothing, Cornelia thought with a frown, except my mother's voice, that is. She hauled herself off the bed and slumped over to her bedroom door. When she peeked through it, she saw her mother standing by the outdoor intercom near the front door.

"Will and Irma are downstairs," Mum called.

"Again?" Cornelia said. In an instant, her sadness grew into a hot burst of rage. She didn't want to see Will, with her all-powerful Heart of Candracar. She didn't want to see Irma, either.

Cornelia knew one thing – she didn't want anything to do with them!

"Tell them I'm out," Cornelia declared to her mother. "I don't feel like seeing them right now."

Cornelia's mother gave her a long, probing look. Cornelia returned the look with a blank stare. Then she turned and stomped back into her room. Before Cornelia clicked her door shut, she heard her mother say into the intercom, "I'm sorry. She won't be back until dinnertime."

Will's voice echoed through the speaker.

"All right, Mrs. Hale," she said. Even through the intercom's fuzzy connection, Cornelia could hear worry in Will's voice. "When she gets in, could you tell her to call us? It's really urgent."

Cornelia closed her bedroom door. She knew better than to let Will's tone of voice get to her.

Everything's always urgent with that group, she thought bitterly. Everything's always one big, crazy drama.

Cornelia cast a sad glance at the flower on her desk.

Beeeeeep!

Cornelia jumped. The buzzer by the front door was beeping again.

What *now?* she wondered grumpily.

"Cornelia!"

Cornelia glared at her bedroom door, then flung it open.

"Whaaaaaat!" she shouted down the stairs. Her mother was standing by the buzzer, one fist planted on her hip.

"Taranee's downstairs," Mum said sharply, "and I'm getting tired of lying to your friends."

"All right, already," Cornelia growled back. This was getting out of control. "Tell her I'll be right there."

Cornelia flounced over to her closet and jammed her feet into a pair of taupe clogs that totally didn't match her long, green skirt. She didn't care. Wondering why her friends insisted on pestering her, she stomped out her apartment door and stewed as she rode down in the elevator to the lobby. She shuffled reluctantly across her building's courtyard toward the locked front gate. Taranee was standing just outside, looking meek and sheepish and, to be honest, a little freaked.

Before she could even register the look on Taranee's face, Cornelia swung the gate open and blurted out, "What do you want?"

"I – I was just passing by," Taranee said, casting her bespectacled eyes downward. "I wanted to say hi."

Cornelia looked up at the sky for a moment, shaking her head in disbelief. Then, she lit into Taranee.

"First the others, and now you!" she sputtered. "What? Did you plan all this? Why won't you just stop pestering me?"

Now Taranee looked more than sheepish. Her wide brown eyes looked scared. They broadcast failure and regret.

But those were emotions Cornelia couldn't deal with.

I've got enough of my own stuff to deal with, she thought. I can't take on Taranee's, too.

So she ignored her impulse to reach out to her friend; to tell Taranee how sad she was feeling and ask her what was wrong in *her* life; to let Taranee give her a comforting hug.

Cornelia was too angry for hugs. At least, that's what she told herself as she slammed the gate in Taranee's face and walked quickly back to her building.

I just want, Cornelia insisted to herself, to be alone!

TWELVE

Irma and Hay Lin crowded in close to Will as the Guardians' leader spoke into the intercom outside Cornelia's building.

"I'm sorry," a woman's voice squawked out of the speaker in the big, silver box. "She won't be back until dinnertime."

"All right, Mrs. Hale," Will replied, her voice wobbling with worry. As Will left her message for Cornelia, Irma shook her head.

It's just like Corny to sit home moping for days not talking to anyone, then be *out* at the moment her friends need her, Irma thought. That's the kind of flaky move Cornelia always pins on *me*.

That is, *if* Cornelia is out doing something fun, Irma thought. But what if she's not?

After all, Taranee was worried about her. She was trying to tell us something about Cornelia in that mental message she sent us at the mall. And it didn't sound like anything good. I still have the pounding headache from that silent scream to prove it.

The moment Will finished speaking with Mrs. Hale, Irma said, "Cornelia's not home. That kind of concerns me."

Will's cheeks went pale and her shoulders began to creep up toward her ears.

That's the Will-Is-Worried pose, Irma thought. She's scared, too. That's *not* a good sign.

Hay Lin was fretting as well. Irma could hear her invisible friend's toe tapping restlessly on the pavement.

Even though she was feeling troubled, Will was still a leader and she had to do something. "There's nothing we can do about Cornelia now," she declared. "So we should focus on tracking Taranee down."

"But where do we even begin to start?" Hay Lin wondered.

"Let's go to my house," Will said with a shrug. "Maybe we can ask the Heart of

Candracar what to do, and then – "

Will choked on her next word, then seemed to forget altogether about completing her sentence. She had just spotted something in the distance. Something scary.

Bracing herself, Irma took her own peek. Bad idea, she thought as soon as she saw what Will had been looking at. She gulped and squeaked, "Look out!"

Walking toward the trio of Guardians was the big, bad goon, with one hand planted on Taranee's back. He seemed to be prodding her along the pavement – and leading her straight toward the girls!

Irma grabbed Hay Lin and Hay Lin grabbed Will. All three girls dashed to hide behind a car parked at the curb. When they peeked out over the hood of the car, it seemed that neither Taranee nor her kidnapper had spotted them.

They were too busy looking up – straight at Cornelia's penthouse apartment.

Irma looked over at Will and cringed. What was going on?

Taranee looked stricken with guilt as she pointed at their friend's home.

"Here we are," she said, reluctantly pointing

to Cornelia's building. "She lives over there."

"I want to see her," the man snapped. "Go call her. I'll wait for you here – and no funny business."

Taranee heaved a huge sigh as the man sauntered to the far corner of the building's wrought-iron fence. He leaned against it cockily.

Casting a fearful glance at her captor, Taranee walked up to the intercom and buzzed Mrs. Hale, asking to see Cornelia.

What will the big, ugly guy do when he finds out Cornelia's not there? Irma wondered. She clenched her jaw to keep her teeth from chattering in fear. The situation kept getting worse!

Irma could have easily gotten herself into a major tizzy if she hadn't been distracted by a sudden motion in the courtyard of Cornelia's building. Somebody was opening the high-rise's dramatic steel-and-glass door and shuffling out into the open.

Irma stared at the person and gasped.

It was Cornelia! A very bedraggled Cornelia, but Cornelia nonetheless. She came down the front walk with a sour scowl on her face. The moment she reached Taranee at the courtyard gate, she started yelling at her.

Irma tuned her out after that. She didn't know what to think. Nor did Hay Lin.

"It's Cornelia!" Hay Lin said in disbelief.

"But her mum just told us she wasn't home," Will whispered. "Cornelia made her mum lie to us!"

"And now," Irma said, "she's yelling at Taranee!"

Slam!

Cornelia had just slammed the metal gate shut, right in Taranee's face.

"Just a minute, Cornelia!" Taranee called out. But Cornelia wouldn't wait even one minute. She stormed back to the building's front door and disappeared into the lobby.

Immediately, Taranee's kidnapper swept over to her side.

"Well done, Taranee," he said mysteriously. "We can go now."

The man began to walk Taranee away. The minute they were out of earshot, Irma turned to Will.

"Cornelia's going to pay for this," she hissed. There was no way she was going to let

Cornelia get away with being so mean. "Why is she being like this?"

"Because she has no idea what's going on!" Will retorted. "We'll explain it all to her later. But for right now we have more important things to do. We've got two hostages to save, and this time, we can't goof up!"

THIRTEEN

Will, Irma, and the still-invisible Hay Lin walked along the pavement, a good half-block behind Taranee and the beady-eyed bald man who had her in his clutches. Will's stomach lurched as she watched Taranee trudge unhappily along next to the man. It reminded her of the last time Taranee had been ripped away from the Guardians. That had happened during the girls' first visit to Metamoor. Prince Phobos and his nasty blue hunter, Frost, had captured Taranee.

Those horrible days when Taranee was imprisoned, Will thought, pressing a hand to her queasy belly, were the only time the five of us have been separated. Until now.

Just before the girls turned the corner in

pursuit of Taranee, Will glanced back at Cornelia's building. Its big, square windows sparkled in the sunshine. The terrace of the top-floor apartment – Cornelia's penthouse – was lush with potted trees and flowering plants.

Normally, Will thought of that sky-scraping garden as warm and inviting. Now, it seemed like a fortress. Cornelia, bitter and lonely, was locked away inside, and Will was starting to worry that she'd never come out.

What happens to the Power of Five then? Will wondered. For that matter, what happens when I move away from Heatherfield? What will become of us?

She still had not told her friends about her mother's plan to move.

Will felt Irma tugging at her sleeve. In her anxiety, Will had been lagging behind. If she didn't pick up the pace, they were in danger of losing Taranee.

Shaking her hair out of her eyes, Will tried to clear her head. There was just too much to handle all at once. She'd have to worry about Cornelia and her own issues later. Right now, it was Taranee who was in trouble.

Just as Will refocused on the thought of helping Taranee, the bald man veered to the right and led Taranee down a cement stairwell on the outside of a building. The three Guardians began to trot after them, careful not to be seen. They didn't want to lose sight of them for a minute, but they had to keep their presence a secret.

When they reached the staircase and peered down the steep steps, Will felt a sinking sensation in her chest.

The stairs led down to the grounds of an old, abandoned factory. A chain-link gate barricaded the property, upon which a sign had been nailed: DANGER.

No kidding, Will thought with a shuddery sigh. She dashed down the stairs and quickly spotted a hole in the fence. Poking her head through it, Will caught sight of Taranee and the man hurrying across a dusty courtyard, then descending another staircase.

"The guy's got some kind of lair in this abandoned factory!" Will told her friends breathlessly. "Come on!"

The three girls climbed through the hole, ran across the large plot of dirt, and tiptoed over to the staircase. If Will hadn't been so scared, she would have laughed out loud at the spylike situation they were in. Peering down the cement steps, Will spotted Taranee. She was just disappearing into the dusky shadows of the dank basement. A moment later, Will couldn't see her anymore, but she was relieved to discover that she could still hear her. Her friend's wispy voice echoed out of the creepy space.

"What is this place?" Taranee asked the man.

"It's a dump, I know," the guy replied, "but I couldn't find anything better. It doesn't matter, though. For your brother, whether it's this place or another place, it wouldn't make a difference."

"Peter!" Taranee screamed.

Will clapped a hand over her mouth to suppress a gasp, then shot Irma and Hay Lin a frightened glance. She motioned toward the bottom of the stairs and both girls nodded. There was no need for Will to do the leadership thing there. All three Guardians felt that they *had* to see what had happened to Taranee's brother.

They crept down the stairs until they could see into the basement. The room was mammoth – a murky, cement cave with cracked floors. It must have been a storage facility once. Now, it was Peter Cook's prison! Taranee's sweet, surfer-dude brother was floating in a giant globe made of sparking, silver magic.

Are we going to have to begin another battle? Will thought with dread. How can we when we are not united? Our power is always strongest when we *are* united. How can we fight when one of our Guardians is stuck in an invisible state and another one is shut away in her bedroom pouting?

Not to mention the Guardian in danger right before Will's very eyes! Taranee was running toward the lethal-looking orb in which Peter was suspended.

"If you don't want to be fried to a crisp," her captor calmly called out to her, "I'd advise you not to get too close to the protection field."

Taranee skidded to a halt, but that didn't stop her from reaching out to her brother with trembling hands. Over her shoulder, she asked the man, "Is he okay?"

"He didn't feel a thing," the man said casually. "And now, I won't be needing your brother anymore. Soon, he'll go back home, completely intact and unharmed."

Then, something began to happen. As the man spoke, his voice started getting raspier and much louder. Will, who had been watching it all unfold, dragged her gaze away from Peter to shoot the kidnapper a quizzical look. She was shocked to see that his voice wasn't the only thing that was changing.

His skin was shifting. In a moment, it had morphed from a pale, putty colour to bright blue!

The man's bald head was suddenly covered by a shock of long, yellow hair, and his muscled back grew broader and more imposing. But it wasn't until two pointy ears sprouted through the creature's long hair that Will finally recognised him.

It's Frost! she thought. Phobos's glorified bloodhound has somehow made it to Heatherfield. Even with his master in prison, he seems intent on continuing to terrorise us.

As if he'd heard Will's very thoughts, Frost bore down on Taranee with a menacing, black-eyed stare and a low growl.

"It's a shame that you and your friends won't be as lucky as your brother," he roared. "*You* will never go home again!"

Will didn't hesitate before making her next move. She barely even had time to think about it. As faulty as the girls' magic might have been at that moment, Will still felt the Heart of Candracar beating inside her. It was as strong as her own pounding heart.

She leapt over the three bottom steps and landed with a thud just behind the evil hunter.

"Are you sure about that, Frost?" she demanded challengingly.

Grunting in surprise, the creature wheeled around and leered at Will and her friends. He lunged for them, but Will ducked beneath his swinging arms, while Irma and Hay Lin vaulted over the banister to land in the center of the room. Taranee ran over to her friends, grinning widely.

"Am I glad to see you!" Taranee cried.

Irma pointed over Taranee's shoulder.

"Yeah, but *he* sure isn't."

Will followed Irma's gaze. Frost was crouched at the bottom of the basement stairs, like a tiger ready to pounce.

"You're mistaken!" he yelled at Irma. "I am glad to see you. I've been waiting for this moment for a long time. Annihilating you will be a great pleasure. Trust me."

Frost began to hurl himself at the Guardians.

That was when Will's magical instincts kicked in. She thrust her right hand out before her and cried, "Heart of Candracar!"

Will clenched her hand in a fist for a moment. When she opened it again, the Heart of Candracar was hovering right above her palm. The crystal orb emitted blinding rays of bright, pink magic. Its power was enough to lift Will's hair from the roots, bathe her friends in a pool of magical beauty, and make Frost shield his own eyes from the Heart's blinding blow. It was the power of all five girls combined.

"Guide us, and protect us in this battle!" she ordered the amulet, in a voice filled with confidence.

From just behind her, Irma piped up, "Yeah, Heart of Candracar! Don't fail us now!"

The glowing orb responded by quickly discharging four glistening teardrops of magic. The silver one shot over to Hay Lin, whirling around

her like a tornado. It whipped her invisible pigtails over her head, tore off her street clothes,
and replaced them with her Guardian's uni-
form: a fluttery split skirt, striped knee socks
and sneakers, a cropped top whose sleeves
curled around her biceps like snakes, and, best
of all, a set of iridescent wings, fluttering from
the center of her back. Hay Lin might have
been a ghostly presence in her invisible state,
but she was still dazzling.

Irma's watery blue magic and Taranee's
orange magic transformed them as well.

And now, Will thought, closing her eyes, it's
my turn.

As her own pink teardrop of magic
corkscrewed around her body, she involuntar-
ily threw her arms over her head. Then she
curled into a ball as magic bubbled up within
her. It suffused her insides, making her feel
warm and buoyant. The feeling shot down her
legs, lengthening them and defining her muscles. Will felt her tousled hair settle into a
shiny, neat style. She knew that her cheek-
bones were sharpening and her eyes were
getting bigger and wiser.

When she became aware of her own purple

skirt swishing around her legs, she threw her head back and straightened out her body.

She was back where she belonged. She was the leader of the Guardians of the Veil, the Keeper of the Heart of Candracar.

The only thing missing, Will thought, glancing at her three beautiful friends, is Cornelia. Without her, this just isn't the same.

Frost had recovered from the Heart of Candracar's blast of light and was surveying the group. He barked out a dismissive laugh.

"Three against one," he scoffed. "I've won against more difficult odds."

Will looked quickly over at Hay Lin. Frost hadn't seen her! That could come in handy.

Hay Lin grinned, too, and shot her friend a thumbs-up.

That *is* a lucky break, Will thought. But is it enough to get us out of this fix? Frost is going to give us the fight of our lives!

As Frost began to lunge at the closest Guardian, Irma, Will flexed her newly strengthened muscles and began conjuring a sphere of magic in her hands. It would be a great weapon for fending Frost off.

But it's not the *perfect* weapon, Will thought

regretfully. *That* would be the Power of Five. Will, Irma, Taranee, Cornelia, and Hay Lin – W.I.T.C.H. – all battling together. As we did when we saved Metamoor.

Is it possible that another save-the-world mission is materialising before our eyes? Will wondered as she watched Irma nimbly dodge Frost's first strike. And will we have the strength to take it on?

Well, she thought with a squint of determination. There's only one way to find out. It's time to conquer Frost.

After that, it's time to face the real challenge – repairing our friendship!

. . . ALWAYS LOOK BEHIND YOU.

OUCH. THAT HAD TO HURT.

THINK HE'S OKAY?

I WOULDN'T WORRY, HAY LIN. THAT MONSTER'S GOT A THICK HIDE.

OHHH!

CRACKZZ KZZ-KZKZZZ ZZ

LOOK! PETER IS BEING SET FREE.

THERE MUST'VE BEEN SOME CONNECTION WITH FROST. WHEN THAT CREEP WAS KNOCKED OUT, THE SPHERE STOPPED WORKING, TOO.

HE'S STILL SLEEPING, BUT OTHERWISE HE LOOKS LIKE HE'S OKAY

GOOD! BUT NOW YOU NEED TO GET YOUR BROTHER OUT OF HERE AND TAKE HIM HOME!

WE'RE GOING TO CANDRACAR! I BET FROST IS EAGER TO SEE HIS OLD FRIENDS, PHOBOS AND CEDRIC!

GULP! TAKE A LOOK AT THE HEART, WILL. IT'S CLOUDED OVER.

YOU'RE RIGHT! SOMETHING'S DEFINITELY WRONG.

YOUR BOND IS NOT AS STRONG AS IT ONCE WAS. YOU LACK A GROUP SPIRIT. AND SOMEONE HAS USED HER POWERS FOR THE WRONG REASONS.

I JUST CAN'T WIN. . . . I'M ALWAYS GETTING YELLED AT.

. . . AND YOU HAVEN'T STOOD BEHIND YOUR FRIEND CORNELIA, WHO'S GOING THROUGH A VERY DIFFICULT TIME.

BUT WE TRIED!

WELL, TRYING ISN'T ENOUGH. YOU'RE BEING TESTED, GUARDIANS.

YOUR POWERS ARE AT THEIR WEAKEST. . . . AND IT'S UP TO YOU TO MAKE THEM STRONG AGAIN.

GOOD LUCK!

NO! PLEASE, WAIT A MINUTE!

WZAM

AAAGH! WHY DON'T WE EVER GET TO FINISH A CONVERSATION? THESE WISE GUYS FROM CANDRACAR ARE REALLY STARTING TO GET ON MY NERVES.